Lover's Instinct

Moon Shifter Series

Katie Reus

SECOND EDITION

About the Book

This wolf is ready to stake his claim...

Shifter Nikan Lawless has it bad for Esperanze Cordona, the sweet and curvy female who only views him as a friend. Lately, however, he's started to see sparks of interest. So when he's assigned to act as her bodyguard during a weekend education conference, he knows it's the perfect opportunity to finally get her to see that they'd be perfect for each other—away from the prying eyes of their pack.

To put his plan into motion, Nikan cancels one of their hotel rooms. Is it underhanded? Yes. But he's playing for keeps with this female. When a dangerous man from Esperanze's past shows up in need of help, Nikan must shield her from a group of rogue shifters and convince her that they're destined to be mates. Since she's a beta and he's an alpha she's afraid things will never work between them. But he knows they're meant to be together and he'll do what it takes to make her his forever.

Chapter 1

Esperanze Cordona rolled her suitcase to the front door of the house she shared with her four—*three*—sisters. For a moment her breath caught in her throat as that familiar pain lanced through her heart. She still couldn't believe Alicia was gone. Didn't know if she'd ever get used to it. Part of her felt guilty for leaving her siblings so soon after their youngest sister's death, but she needed to get out of the house and away from her entire pack.

Just for the weekend. One of her former professors was giving a lecture in DC and she hadn't seen him in close to thirty years—since before shifters and other paranormal beings had come out to the world two decades ago—so this was the perfect opportunity. While she respected his work and wanted to see him, the truth was, she just needed to get away from the ranch. Maybe it would dull her pain.

As she opened the front door, she immediately smiled. Pain from thoughts of her dead sister lingered in her heart, but seeing Nikan Lawless on her doorstep soothed some of it. From the moment they'd become friends, she'd noticed his calming effect on everyone, herself included. The tall, dark-haired, bronze skinned shifter might be part of the warrior class, but he was incredibly laid-back.

Thanks to his Native American ancestry, the sharp planes of his face and high cheekbones would make him an artist's dream. She dabbled in photography and was working her way up to asking him if she could photograph him. Every day for the past few weeks she'd found herself looking forward to their nightly walks and conversation, but hadn't found the right moment. "Hey, you caught me on my way out."

"I know. I'm going with you." His deep voice was so unique she'd be able to pick it out of a crowd of thousands.

She blinked, sure she'd misheard him. She'd just seen him last night and he hadn't said anything. "What? Why?"

A casual shrug of those incredibly broad shoulders. "Connor's orders."

"I don't understand. The pack can't afford to lose you for the weekend." Over the past few months their pack had undergone some serious changes and threats from outsiders. Before Connor and his small, all male pack of warriors had united with theirs, Esperanze's pack had lost almost two dozen members, including all the males, to poisoning. That combined with a human element known as the Antiparanormal League who had been wreaking havoc on their pack meant her packmates needed all the security available at the ranch.

His full mouth quirked up at the corners, giving him what some females of the pack considered an irresistible quality. "I'm glad you think so highly of my abilities, but they'll survive without me."

Rolling her eyes, she shook her head and pulled her suitcase out behind her before shutting the door. "It's just a weekend trip. I'll be fine by myself and I don't need a babysitter."

"Trust me, Essie, I don't want to be your babysitter." He often called her Essie instead of Esperanze and for some annoying reason it always made her heart beat just a little faster.

She wasn't sure why the tall, broad shifter had befriended her, but she was glad he had. She hadn't had many male friends who weren't academics so it surprised her how much she and this warrior had in common. "Then tell Connor that. I'm sure if he hears it from you that you don't want to go on this trip—"

"I never said that either." He lifted her suitcase with the kind of ease that reminded her exactly how different they were.

Where she was a beta—one of the physically weakest of the pack—he was not only an alpha shifter in nature, he was a warrior, born to protect the pack. "So you *want* to go with me to DC?"

Instead of responding, he turned and strode across the yard toward the parking structure where most of the pack kept their vehicles. For a split second she contemplated arguing with him, but he had a stubborn look in his dark eyes that told her it would be pointless. Not to mention she loved his company. She followed him and slid into the passenger seat of his truck while he loaded her stuff into the extended cab. Before she could settle in, he'd opened her door and was strapping her in. The intimate way he leaned closer, brushing his chest against her breasts, stunned her.

She wanted to stop her physical reaction but couldn't. Her heart rate increased as his spicy, sandalwood scent twined around her in an almost seductive embrace. Though she would never admit it, she'd had a couple fantasies about what it would be like to have his strong, muscular body naked and covering hers. Immediately she chastised herself. Nikan was her friend. Nothing more. She'd seen the way her female cousins looked at him. And they were all alphas, much more his type.

"For the record, I want to be anywhere you are," he murmured in her ear, so close he might as well have run his tongue along it.

That thought sent a shiver snaking through her but then she felt stupid. Men like Nikan didn't go for women like her. It was one thing to be friends but another to be lovers. He occasionally flirted with her but she was pretty sure it was just innocent.

Before she could catch her breath or even respond, he'd pulled away and shut the door. Only then did she allow herself to push out a long pent up breath. Suddenly the impending trip to Washington, DC, seemed unbearably long.

Just because she had a teeny tiny crush on Nikan didn't mean anything. They were friends, nothing more. She wasn't stupid enough to fall for an alpha. Her own mother had done that and it was something Esperanze had vowed never to repeat. Not after seeing the unbalanced relationship of her parents. As Nikan pulled out of the parking structure, she turned on the radio before settling back against the seat. She could get through this weekend just fine. It wasn't as if he'd be going with her everywhere.

Chapter 2

"What do you mean you only have one room booked?" Esperanze's voice was civil as she spoke to the woman behind the hotel's reservation desk, but Nikan bit back a smile as she tried to contain her annoyance. He knew she had a temper underneath that buttoned up exterior and he wanted to see it.

"I'm sorry, ma'am. With the conference being held next door we're booked solid and something must have happened to one of the room reservations. I'll be happy to call around and find another hotel for you. I'm so sorry—"

"That won't be necessary," Nikan interjected.

Esperanze swiveled to look at him. "What do you mean it won't be necessary? There's only one bed."

"It's a king-sized bed. I can keep my hands to myself if you can." He dropped his voice a couple octaves and forced himself not to smile when her cheeks flushed bright red.

She opened her mouth but nothing came out, so he gently nudged her aside and finished dealing with the woman at the front desk. It was certainly no mistake that they only had one room. He'd called ahead and cancelled his adjoining room.

Sneaky? Definitely. If that's the way he had to play it to get sweet and sexy Esperanze to pay attention to him, he had no problem with slightly underhanded tactics. He'd admit what he'd done later. Maybe.

This friends-only thing was getting old. He loved being her friend but wanted a hell of a lot more. At first he'd thought she was just teasing him, that her coyness was part of their courting before he took her as his mate. After a few weeks he'd realized that she wasn't coy, just oblivious to the effect she had on him.

It was like a hunger growing inside him, clawing and needy every time she was near. He'd kill for just a taste of her and when he'd heard she was going away to this conference—away from the pack and her sisters—he knew it was the perfect chance for them to be alone together.

As they strode to the elevators he couldn't help but sneak looks at her. Her waist length dark hair fell in soft waves down her back. Most of the females of their pack had much shorter hair, a symbol of the changing times and their embracement of human styles, but not Esperanze. He wouldn't change a thing about her, especially not that gorgeous hair. He wanted to run his fingers through it while she rode him, wrap his hands around it while she—

"What?" she demanded.

He blinked, and found himself staring into her very annoyed green eyes. "Uh, what?"

"You're staring. Do I have something on my face?"

When he shook his head she let out an exasperated sigh and punched the "up" button again. As she did, she muttered under her breath about the stupid hotel. Once they stepped into the elevator he could barely contain his groan. Her sweet exotic scent wrapped around him. It reminded him of coconuts and the beach. Of lying on the sand and indulging in lazy, playful sex.

"... and it's not as if you have to come with me tonight. The first lecture—"

"I'm coming with you." He had no idea what she'd been talking about but he was going wherever she was.

"But why? You'll be bored out of your mind." Her brow knitted together as she turned to stare up at him.

When the elevator dinged and the doors whooshed open, he stepped out first to make sure there wasn't a threat in the hallway. Danger was unlikely, but some things were ingrained so deeply in him, he couldn't change his need to protect.

Continuing to frown, she stepped out after him and practically stomped down the hallway toward their room. He followed with their suitcases and just enjoyed the view of her tight backside. Before this weekend was over he was going to have his first taste of her. The first of many as far as he was concerned. He'd show her so much pleasure she'd have no doubt that he wanted more than friendship.

Then he'd convince her he wanted forever.

Chapter 3

Esperanze slid her mascara wand into its holder then twisted it shut. Done. And by a quick glance at her slim watch, time to go. She didn't want to be late for the first lecture.

As she opened the bathroom door and stepped into the hotel room she found Nikan lounging against the giant bed. The bed they were supposedly going to be sharing later that night. Yeah, she'd just see about that.

As usual, his dark hair was secured at his neck with a thin black hair tie and his long, muscular legs were stretched out on the mattress. With one arm propped up behind his head as he leaned against the headboard watching the muted television, he looked casual, relaxed. But she knew better. His other hand rested lightly over the weapon she knew was covered by his black leather jacket. Not that he'd need it even if they were attacked. As a member of the warrior class, he'd have no problem taking on most beings, human or supernatural.

He flicked a glance her way, then froze, his dark eyes widening.

Immediately her throat clenched and a wave of self-conscious-ness swept over her. Maybe she shouldn't have worn the fitted green dress, should have gone with a staid skirt suit instead. Almost everyone at these educational conferences dressed the same. She glanced down at herself. "Is it too much for a lecture?"

"No." He was up and on his feet before she could blink. "You look fucking gorgeous."

Oh my. "Uh, thanks." She felt her cheeks flush then immediately cursed her silly reaction. Looking away, she unzipped the top part of her suitcase and pulled out her five-inch black peep-toe pumps. It was cold and would make more sense for her to wear boots, but she didn't care. At the ranch it was ridiculous for her to dress up, so she usually wore boring boots. And boring, practical clothes. Not this weekend. After slipping on the pumps, she put on her knee length wool pea coat and cinched the belt tight around her waist.

When she turned back around she found Nikan mere inches in front of her, staring down at her with something in his eyes she wasn't sure how to define. Wasn't sure she wanted to. But if she had to, he looked hungry. For her. Fear sparked inside her for a brief moment. He was bigger and stronger than she and could do any damn thing he wanted. Not that her inner wolf worried he would, but past experience told her bigger, stronger wolves sometimes used their size and strength to intimidate beta wolves. Just because she was physically weaker didn't mean she didn't have a mind of her own.

She wasn't sure if he sensed her unease, but Nikan immediately backed off. Maybe he'd scented her fear. Whatever it was, when he moved away, it eased her stress.

As she grabbed her clutch from the bed, Nikan's deep voice rolled over her. "I would never hurt you, Essie."

She swallowed hard, feeling guilty and a little stupid for her momentary burst of panic. "I know that. Why would you even say that?" Nerves made her rush on and start babbling like she always did when she was anxious. She hurried toward the door and jerked it open, still talking as they headed toward the elevators. "I'm just excited about this lecture. I haven't seen Professor Kelly in thirty years. He was human and so much younger than me at least in actual years, but I used to have the biggest crush on him. His mind was so far beyond his peers. At the time he was studying thermodynamics, and for one brief semester in college I thought I might go into physics too, but in the end knew education was it for me. That's why it's so nice to have little ones on the ranch again, even if they do get annoyed with their homework."

As they stopped in front of the elevators she ordered her mouth to stop running. When she glanced at Nikan he had an almost dark expression on his face. "You had a crush on your professor?"

She blinked at his question. "What? Oh, yeah, a long time ago." She started to say more when the doors opened. They were both silent as they joined the young human couple inside.

Nikan was quiet the rest of the walk through the lobby, outside and as they strode toward the hotel next door. He was slightly tense and she had a feeling he was going to be more so once they reached the room where the lecture was being held. She'd left out one tiny detail when she'd told her Alpha about this conference, and no one had thought to check it out because, well, why would they? She was an adult and could make decisions for herself. So what if this conference was being hosted by vampires? They were all academics and she'd received an invitation.

As they stepped into the lobby of the hotel next door, she could feel Nikan's entire demeanor change. Without even looking at him, it was like a switch flipped inside him.

"Esperanze," he murmured, low enough for only her to hear. "We need to leave, *now*."

She swallowed hard and glanced up at him. "No, we don't."

His dark gaze was sharp and assessing. "I don't think you understand."

Oh, she understood perfectly well. Warriors had an innate sense of danger whereas betas still had that innate animal sense, but less honed. He likely assumed she couldn't sense the vampires. "I probably should have told you, but, uh, this conference is being hosted by vampires. But they're not the only paranormal beings here. There are supposed to be a few fae, other shifters—lupine, ursine and feline—and I even heard there were a few half-demons attending." She'd never met a demon before and was hoping to. As of twenty years ago humans knew of the existence of shifters and vampires but they didn't know about all paranormal beings, especially not demons.

Nikan's hand was gripping her upper arm and he hadn't let them take another step past the immediate inner area of the lobby. "You knew about this but didn't tell Connor? Or *me*?"

She bit her bottom lip and tried to squash the guilt building inside of her. "I didn't think he'd let me go."

His expression darkened. "Damn right he wouldn't have. And I wouldn't have either. We're leaving right now." He increased his grip, but not so much that it hurt. Just so he made his point.

She dug her heels in. "No, we're not. You can go if you want, but I'm staying. I'm not a child and I don't need your protection. And I sure as hell don't need your permission. I didn't ask for you to come and if you don't like it, you know where the exit is."

His lips parted, as if she'd surprised him. Which she probably had. Betas weren't known for mouthing off. Didn't mean they couldn't. "Essie," he murmured, low and sensual, and ran his hand down her arm, caressing her in a soft, inviting manner.

Her abdomen clenched with impossible need until she realized what he was doing. She growled softly. "That's pretty low. If you think you can charm me into leaving because of your sexuality, you don't know me at all." That he'd even try stung. They were friends. She wrenched her arm away.

He opened his mouth but was cut off by the sound of a male voice calling out her name. They both turned and she immediately smiled at the tall, auburn haired man striding toward them. Antoine Kelly was just as she remembered him. Taller than her, though a couple inches shorter than Nikan. With a lean build and pale skin, he would have blended into the vampire community even before he'd been turned.

"You look just as beautiful as I remember." Her former professor lightly kissed her on both cheeks before embracing her.

Next to her Nikan growled deep in his throat, and she turned to find him glaring at Antoine. His expression was so dark she was glad it wasn't directed at her.

Her former professor stepped back and held out a friendly hand to Nikan. "I'm Antoine Kelly. Are you two mated? I didn't realize—"

"We're not mated, just friends." She gently elbowed Nikan, hoping he'd wipe that expression off his face that said he was about to decapitate her old friend.

Antoine raised an eyebrow and gave her a look that said he didn't quite believe her. Since Nikan didn't return his handshake—she wanted to throttle him for that!—Antoine let his hand drop.

Thankfully he wasn't intimidated by the man next to her. "After my lecture a few of us are getting together for drinks downtown. It's a place that caters to supernatural beings. I'd love it if both of you would join me."

"Of course," she said before Nikan could reject him.

They made small talk for a few minutes, but Antoine eventually excused himself, probably because of the death glares Nikan was giving him. Once her friend was out of earshot, she nudged Nikan in the ribs with her elbow. "You acted like a child."

The tall shifter just shrugged and placed his hand at the small of her back. "We should probably hurry if you want a good seat." He motioned toward the open doors where others were already heading inside.

Pausing, she grasped his forearm. She wasn't inclined to complain, but he'd given in way too easily. "Why are you being so acquiescent?"

"Maybe I just don't want you mad at me." She snorted and he shrugged again in that maddeningly casual way of his. "Okay, maybe I've assessed that of all the paranormal beings I've seen and scented so far, none of them are real threats."

That made sense, but she was still annoyed with him. "So we're not going to talk about the way you just acted toward my friend?"

He shrugged. "I don't like vampires."

"Apparently. Do you think you can act civil when we go out tonight?"

"I've never claimed to be civil," he said with a soft growl, flashing his canines.

After the way her mother had been bullied by her father she'd be damned if she let anyone do the same to her, especially not someone she considered a friend. "I don't know what your problem is, but keep it up and we're not friends anymore." Without waiting for a response, she turned on her heel and stalked toward the open doors.

Let Nikan stew on that. She wasn't going to allow anyone to intimidate her because of his strength. She completely understood pack rules and her place in the hierarchy, but that didn't mean she had less worth or didn't deserve to be treated with respect.

Chapter 4

As the last lecturer finally stopped talking, Nikan allowed a fraction of relief to slide into his veins. There were almost one hundred individuals in the giant hotel conference room. Esperanze hadn't been wrong about the various types of paranormal creatures. Shifters of all varieties, fae, more than a handful of demons and even some humans. But vamps definitely outnumbered everyone else.

From what he'd assessed, only a few of the vampires were of the vamp warrior class. He could tell because of the power they put off. Like energy pulsing through the air, it could be felt by all supernaturals. Right now he only sensed three with high levels of power. It made him feel a little better, but not much. He didn't like Esperanze being so near all these other creatures, and he knew why.

His inner wolf wanted to protect her, keep her safe, and until they mated—hell, *if* they mated—the need inside him wouldn't go away. The most primal part of him needed to mark her, to let the world know she was his. Until that happened, he knew the edginess pumping through him wouldn't ease.

Esperanze lightly clutched his forearm as they stood. Some of her annoyance had faded during the speeches, and for that he was thankful. He knew because of the touch. She did it all the time, and he guessed she wasn't even aware of it. But she often made skin-to-skin contact with him, and it soothed his wolf more than he'd ever imagined possible. While it might calm him, just the feel of her long, elegant fingers resting on his arm made him think about what it would be like to have those fingers curled around another part of his body.

"There are a few people I want to talk to before we leave. Do you want to wait for me or would you mind meeting them?" Her question was so damn polite, it rankled him. What did she think, that he'd actually leave her?

He placed his hand over hers. "I'm not leaving your side."

Her cheeks flushed that delicate shade of pink that made him want to groan. Unable to stop himself he reached out and tucked a dark strand of hair behind her ear. When his knuckles grazed her cheekbone, she sucked in a breath. That exotic, coconut scent of hers intensified, and he almost jerked back.

Was she turned on?

Before he could contemplate what the scent meant, it registered that a vaguely familiar female voice had said his name.

"Nikan!"

He turned at the sound, surprised to see Maya Morgan striding toward him. Tall, blond, built like an athlete, she practically launched herself at him, pulling him into a tight embrace. He hadn't seen her in almost forty years. After hugging her, he stepped back and tried to put a little distance between them but she splayed her fingers across his chest. "What are you doing here?"

He nodded at Esperanze, who was giving him the oddest look. "This is my packmate, Esperanze. She was invited to this conference. I'm her guard for the weekend."

Esperanze's eyes narrowed at him with pure anger for a fraction of a second. It was gone so quick he could almost pretend he'd imagined it, but he knew what he'd seen. Just as quickly she smiled politely at the other lupine shifter. "Nice to meet you."

Maya nodded once then slightly sniffed the air as she looked between them. The action was slight but he knew what she was trying to ascertain. Her question solidified it. "Are you two mated?"

Before he could answer, Esperanze shook her head. "No. If you two will excuse me, I see someone I'd like to speak to."

Nikan wanted to go after her, but Maya grabbed onto his arm and jumped into a diatribe of questions. She wanted to know what he'd been doing the last forty years, how long he'd been part of Connor Armstrong's pack and why he wasn't mated yet. The pretty shifter made it clear she'd be interested in some fun while he was in town, but all his focus was on one woman.

At the moment, that woman was hugging another male. A shifter this time. From deep inside a growl started, but he shoved it back. The mere sight was making Nikan's predatory nature claw at the surface. He wanted some alone time with Esperanze, and fast. He was edgy and restless as hell. This was one of the reasons he hated cities. Nowhere to shift and run free when he needed it.

Right now his beast was demanding to be unleashed, to let off steam, but he knew even that wouldn't help his real problem. Nothing could do that but finally marking Esperanze as his.

Chapter 5

Esperanze slid onto the barstool of one of the small side bars in the three-story place called The Blue Moon as Nikan ordered their drinks. Electric blue lights illuminated the three bars on the first floor and other bright colors splashed the dance floor from the overhead lighting.

A steady beat of music pumped through the speakers but it wasn't too loud. Most supernatural beings had extrasensory abilities, so overamplified music would have killed their ears. Her old professor had been right. This place definitely catered to paranormal beings. If the softer music wasn't her first clue, it would be the blood donors walking around, offering themselves up to hungry vampires. It was obvious they were there of their own free will and Esperanze had a feeling they were paid incredibly well. And some of them probably got off on it.

She glanced up at Nikan, a smile playing on her face. "This place is interesting."

"Not my style," he murmured, his dark gaze catching hers.

Instantly her stomach tightened and she didn't know what to do about it. She'd been trying to deny her feelings for Nikan for weeks. She'd seen the impact being married to an alpha had had on her now deceased beta mother. But her parents had never been friends, not like the way she and Nikan were. That reminder increased her guilt about what she'd said to him before the lectures. "I'm sorry I said we wouldn't be friends anymore."

To her surprise, an easy grin lit his face as he fully turned to face her. Tugging her stool closer, he stopped only when their knees touched. "I don't blame you. I was kind of a jackass."

Returning his smile, she shrugged. "I won't argue with you there."

"Hey, now." He tweaked her nose and she felt herself flush.

"So were you completely bored?"

He shook his head, his face serious. "Your former professor was interesting. The other two lecturers..." A shrug.

She loved that he wouldn't say anything bad about the other speakers. "You're too nice. The other two were *awful*. The context was interesting, but their voices were so monotone I thought I was going to fall asleep."

"So why aren't you speaking?"

"Other than having a deathly fear of speaking in public, this convention is focused on the sciences. I just came because I thought it would be interesting. And, yes, I know that makes me a total geek." She wasn't embarrassed though.

"I like geeks." There was a note in his voice that made her pause.

The bartender placed their drinks in front of them. The tension in her chest loosened as she turned to take her chocolate martini. And no surprise, Nikan had settled on a beer. For the past few weeks he'd been stopping by her house almost every night that he wasn't on patrol, and she'd quickly learned his favorite brand of beer. She hadn't even been conscious of it at first, but she'd eventually realized she'd changed her shopping patterns to buy stuff she knew he'd like.

And to give him credit, he'd never stopped by the house she lived in with her sisters at the ranch empty-handed. Whether it was flowers, wine or other little gifts, he always brought something for her and her sisters. Never specifically for her, but for everyone.

"What are you thinking of?" Nikan nudged her with his knee, pulling her out of her thoughts.

Esperanze paused, thinking of how to phrase her question. When she'd seen that woman from the conference touching him all proprietarily it had brought out her claws. Literally. She'd escaped so Nikan wouldn't see her physical reaction. Finally she decided to go with what was on her mind. "I appreciate how you bring gifts to our house every time you come by, but..." She felt herself start to stumble over her words and struggled to rephrase, "Are you... Do you only bring them just for us or do you stop by, uh, any of my cousins' homes?" She meant her female alpha cousins, any of whom would be a much better fit for this giant warrior.

Nikan leaned closer, that sandalwood scent teasing her nose as he enclosed her legs with his. "Everything I bring is for you. I like your sisters, but the gifts for them are only because it makes you happy."

His words wrapped around her like the sweetest caress. Her heart pounded wildly in her chest. When his gaze zeroed in on her lips, she instinctively moistened them, then cursed herself for the action, knowing it looked like an invitation.

Nikan growled, the sound low and throaty, and she felt it all the way to her toes. For a brief moment she wondered what it would feel like to have his lips teasing hers, to have his body pressed to hers, to wrap her legs around him and feel his erection pushing against the wet heat of her core.

Surprised by the sudden sway of her thoughts she jerked back, her gaze flying to his. Dark eyes looked at her, as if he was waiting for something. She pressed a light hand to his chest, her fingers curling slightly against the broad expanse of his muscle. The man was certainly built, something she knew, but actually feeling all that power under her fingertips made the most animalistic part of her flare to life. She squashed it back down. "Nikan, we're friends. I don't want to lose our friendship." He might not have been in her life that long but she couldn't imagine it without him now. If they did something stupid, like kiss, it would definitely lead to more and that would ruin everything. Dropping her hand, she leaned back, putting more distance between them.

"I don't want to lose our friendship either," he rasped out, his voice unsteady. "Why can't we be friends and... more?"

"Because it wouldn't last and then things would get awkward once it ended." She had no doubt things would inevitably end and she didn't want to be in an unequal relationship, not when she'd seen what could happen. Of course, Nikan had never treated her like she was inferior, but she knew how things worked.

He reached out, gently cupped her cheek and slowly rubbed his thumb over her skin. "Essie—"

"I need to use the restroom. Please excuse me." She knew she sounded overly formal but she desperately needed to escape. Her skin was on fire where he'd stroked her and if she stayed her resolve might crumble. Sliding off the chair, she ducked underneath his arm.

When he touched her, it was almost impossible to think straight. And when he stared at her as if she was the only thing that mattered, it created an ache deep inside her chest, making her wish things were different.

Weaving her way through high-top bar tables and other patrons, she only stopped once she was inside a restroom with five stalls. The room was plush, with marble countertops and a place to sit and lounge—as if she wanted to hang out in there—and she immediately made her way to one of the sinks and splashed cold water on her face.

It did nothing to cool the burning need thrumming through her veins. She'd tried to deny her growing feelings for Nikan from the moment they'd met. Had ignored comments her sisters made about their friendly relationship. But when he looked at her as if he'd like to devour her, to lick and kiss every inch of her body, she couldn't deny the heat between them any longer. It was real and growing hotter every second she was around him.

Cursing her own cowardice, she dried her face and headed out. Running away was stupid and she owed it to him to sit and talk and get things back on an even footing. Making her way through the growing crowd, she nearly stumbled when she saw that same woman from the conference talking to Nikan at the bar. The blonde's hand was on his chest again.

Instantly Esperanze's claws unsheathed, making her almost drop her purse. Taking a deep breath, she forced herself to focus. She wasn't a pup, she was an eighty-year-old lupine shifter who'd been in control of her wolf since she was ten. Whoever this female was, she was about to learn Nikan wasn't available.

Not allowing herself to dwell on what her possessive thoughts meant for the future, she headed toward them. Before she'd taken two steps, Antoine appeared from the crowd and pulled her to a stop.

"Esperanze, I'm so glad you came." He almost sounded out of breath.

Turning to her former mentor, she smiled despite her newly dark mood. She would have been surprised that she hadn't scented him, but the place was packed and she was distracted. "Of course. Your directions were very easy."

Antoine tugged at the collar of his shirt nervously. "I need to talk to you about something. In private," he murmured.

Concerned by his gray pallor, she nodded and followed him up a short set of stairs to a semiprivate area. A heavy velvet curtain was pulled back by a thick cord to reveal a rounded booth and table. He slid onto one side so she sat on the other. The moment they'd taken seats, a woman wearing a skirt that just barely covered her crotch, a bikini style top and a studded collar approached the table. She greeted Antoine warmly as if she knew him. "It's good to see you, Antoine. Do you need my services?"

Esperanze raised an eyebrow at the word "services" as he shook his head and told the woman they wanted to be alone. "How has the transition been?" she asked the moment the woman was out of earshot, worried it had something to do with his vampirism.

"The past couple decades have been good, but..." Trailing off, he scrubbed a hand over his face. The action was so out of character it made Esperanze falter. Antoine had been turned when he was forty-two by a former vampire lover who had adored him. Though he'd always looked young, he had a boyish charm about him, which was why he was still friends with the female who had changed him even though they were no longer involved. But tonight his blue eyes held too much pain, aging him.

"What's going on?"

"I got into some trouble and—"

As Antoine suddenly stopped talking, she found herself being tugged into Nikan's lap. She hadn't even heard or seen him move into the booth. His dark eyes were slightly dilated. Something wild and hungry lurked in their depths. "What are you doing?" she asked.

He opened his mouth, flashing his canines, but didn't look at her. Instead he focused on Antoine. "Leave us," he growled.

Esperanze placed a hand on his chest, alarm churning inside her. "Nikan—"

"It's okay, Esperanze. Call me later tonight. I need to talk, but it can wait." She heard Antoine moving behind her then the thick curtain that had been pulled back fell into place, blocking them from everything.

"Why are you in one of these alcoves with him?" Nikan asked, his voice deep and almost angry. One of his hands clenched on her hipbone, holding her tight, while the other one encircled her waist.

She splayed both hands on his shoulders smoothing them down. His proprietary behavior shocked her. Something wasn't right with Nikan and her inner wolf needed to soothe him. "He just wanted to talk," she murmured, keeping her voice low.

"Maya told me what these places are used for." He followed up with another growl.

Even though her wolf told her he needed calming, anger sparked inside her. She didn't know what they were used for but had a pretty good idea at the mention of the other female shifter. "Maya? Did she invite you to join her in one?"

"Yes," he snapped.

She narrowed her eyes. "Then why aren't you with her?"

"Because I only want you!" His breathing was harsh, uneven and it appeared as if he might actually lose control of his beast.

Her heart hammered against her chest. The raw need in his voice stunned her. She'd seen Nikan in shifted form before and he was huge. Beautiful, but still very large. From the way he was acting she was afraid what would happen if he shifted forms. Reaching up, she gently cupped his cheeks, caging his gorgeous face in with her hands. "I was only in here because Antoine wanted to talk about something. The curtain was left open, in case you didn't notice."

At the mention of the curtain his gaze flicked away for a moment before he turned back to her. "It's closed now."

The invitation was clear in his voice. One she knew she should ignore, but God help her, she couldn't. Not when he looked almost lost as he stared at her. Moving her hand from his cheek, she reached around and pulled the black tie free from his hair, letting his dark, thick mane free. Most of the males of their pack had short, military style cuts, but not Nikan. She loved that he wore it just above his shoulders. Threading her fingers through it, she leaned a fraction closer.

"What exactly did you have in mind?" she whispered even though she doubted anyone could hear them. The curtain had to be thicker than it looked because she could barely hear the music outside it. Nerves fluttered through her. Making this kind of move was so out of character for her, but she knew Nikan would keep her safe. Even if she ended up regretting what happened tonight—though the most primal part of her told her she wouldn't—she couldn't stop herself.

The hand on her hip tightened then slid lower until he reached the hem of her dress. He held her captured with his dark eyes, waiting for her response.

She wasn't sure exactly what he wanted, but she knew her answer would probably be yes to whatever it was. Swallowing hard, she nodded her assent, an answer to whatever unspoken question he was asking.

His callused fingers played against her leg as his hand moved under her dress. He was watching her, a hungry expression on the sharp planes of his face. The higher he went, the heavier her eyelids grew. She felt almost drugged. He stopped a few inches short of the juncture between her thighs and just lightly stroked her skin.

The teasing action had her entire body tightening with desire. Since he hadn't moved she leaned forward, covering the distance between them, but he took over. On a growl, he took her mouth, teasing with his lips and tongue. Not so gently, he tugged her bottom lip between his teeth as his fingers tightened on one of her inner thighs.

"I want to take you right here, Essie," he whispered against her mouth.

His voice was as unsteady as her shaking insides. This was a different side to Nikan. He had a wild, uncontrollable look to him and with his hair down, even more so. But she wasn't afraid. He'd never physically hurt her. Of that she was absolutely sure. Still, this was moving too fast. "I'm not ready... for that." She wasn't sure that she'd ever be ready to completely surrender to this man. And she knew that's what he would ultimately want.

"I know, but I still want to pleasure you," he said softly.

Her insides melted a little at his words. "Nikan." Her fingers tightened on his shoulders as she tried to pull him closer. As long as she knew they could stop at any moment, she didn't want to stop kissing him.

The angle was awkward and as she tried to turn so that her body was more facing his, he took over. Withdrawing his hand from her thigh, he grabbed her hips and moved her so that she had no choice but to straddle him. But her dress was too tight. Before she could shimmy it up, the back seam ripped. The material bunched upward under the force, exposing more of her legs. A small voice in her head told her she should be shocked and should probably stop things, but she trusted Nikan. He wouldn't push her more than she was ready for.

"I'll buy you a new one." His lips brushed against her neck before he nuzzled right below her ear.

Esperanze shuddered when he raked his teeth along her skin, following with his lips. He exerted enough pressure that she thought he might break the skin, but then he eased and licked her with his tongue and pressed his lips to his almost-bites. The sensation was wildly erotic.

She felt so exposed like this, but he cradled her close to his body. Even with their clothing between them, she savored the feel of her breasts against his chest. Everywhere he touched, kissed and licked left a blaze of scorching heat in its path. She wanted more. Being away from the ranch made her uninhibited. Even though she knew they were taking a big chance at ruining their friendship, everything about this moment seemed right. So right it scared her a little that he might see this as only a physical or onetime thing, not a prelude to more.

Reaching between their bodies, she began sliding her hand down his covered chest, intent on grasping the erection she felt pressing against her belly. Lightning fast, one of his hands encircled her wrist to stop her.

He pulled his head back so she could see his face. His dark eyes practically sparked with lust. "Don't touch me. Not now." His deep voice shook.

"Why?" Her fingers flexed as his grip on her wrist tightened.

He didn't answer. Instead, he reached between her legs and cupped her mound in a completely possessive manner. Even though she was covered, the action took her so off guard she jerked against his hand. When she did, he pressed the heel of his palm against her clit with a perfect amount of pressure. Her inner walls automatically clenched with the need to be filled by him.

This is way too soon. The words sounded loudly in her head, but she ignored them.

It took a moment for it to set in that Nikan was touching her so intimately. They'd gone from petting and kissing to a very intimate embrace so quickly she struggled to wrap her mind around it. He didn't give her a chance to dwell on what they were doing.

Moving the flimsy material aside, he didn't stop until his rough palm was on her most delicate skin and one of his fingers was pushing inside her. Lifting up on her knees, she held the back of his head with one hand and kept a death grip on his shoulder with the other. "What are you doing?" Okay, not exactly the brightest question. It just slipped out from sheer nervousness. This was such a huge step they were taking.

"Let me do this for you." His gaze was intense as he looked up at her. When he began moving his finger inside her, she lost all ability to think. He moved slowly at first, exploring what she liked, what made her shudder. It didn't take long for him to figure it out.

Letting her head fall back, she tried to hold on to some of her control but knew it was a losing battle. His finger slid in and out of her in a steady rhythm that drove her crazy with need. Her breasts felt heavy and her nipples tightened to almost painful points. If they weren't in such a semipublic place she would shed all her clothes. Hell, she was tempted to do it anyway. Knowing someone could walk in on them at any moment was incredibly erotic and so unlike her.

Without warning he tore his mouth from where he was nibbling her neck and crushed his lips to hers. His tongue stroked and danced with hers in a similar rhythm to the way he was working his finger inside her. As a sudden image of his head between her legs flooded her brain, she rolled her hips against him.

He increased his movements and began stroking her clit with his thumb with such perfect precision it scared her. It was as if he was completely attuned to her body. When he nipped her bottom lip she allowed herself to just let go even though a small voice in her head told her to hold on to some of her control. Her orgasm was swift and sharp, pulsing through her in sweeping waves. The pleasure swirled everywhere, touching all her nerve endings until finally she went limp in his arms.

Nikan embraced her, pulling her tight against his chest. Still propped up over him, she wrapped her arms around him, threading her fingers through his hair as she held his head to her chest and caught her breath.

Her heart beat out of control even though she was coming down from her climax. Luckily, she could feel his heartbeat and it was just as erratic as hers.

She wasn't sure how long they stayed there, holding each other, but when she heard music much clearer, she realized someone was pulling the curtain back, allowing sound in.

"This booth is occupied!" Nikan snarled and immediately the curtain fell back into place.

But it had broken the intimate moment. Swallowing hard, she leaned back to look at him. His expression was unreadable, but when he reached up and cupped her cheek, some of her tension drained away. She desperately hoped things wouldn't get awkward between them especially since she had no idea what this meant for their future.

Chapter 6

Even though he didn't want to let her go, Nikan helped Esperanze off his lap and tugged her dress down until it covered her legs. Not that it mattered since he'd completely ripped it up the back. At least she had her coat, which she was cinching tightly around her waist. He wanted to get her back to the hotel room where they'd have more privacy. Immediately. Not only did he want to show her more pleasure, he wanted to make it clear this wasn't just a physical thing for him.

When she glanced up, her fingers froze on the belt she'd just tied. Her green eyes were so expressive and not for the first time he thought she'd be an awful poker player. Right now she looked confused. Before he could stop himself, he pulled her back onto his lap and wrapped his arm tight around her waist.

Which was what had gotten him into trouble in the first place. Not that he'd take back what had just happened between them. Especially since he could scent her on him, surrounding him. It was intoxicating. When Maya had invited him to one of the roped off booths Nikan had seen Esperanze disappear into with that fucking vampire, he'd left Maya without a word. He'd been unable to stop himself from following after *his Essie* once he'd realized what the booths were used for. It had taken all his restraint not to mark her right here, to sink his teeth in to her neck, putting his scent on her for everyone to know she was claimed. He'd come close a few times, raking his teeth over her delicate skin.

But he respected her enough to wait to ask for permission. Well, his human side did. His wolf just wanted to take. "You look gorgeous when you come."

Her cheeks flushed crimson, but at least she laughed. The throaty sound speared straight through his heart. "I can't believe you just said that." The flush spread down to her neck, but she didn't hide her face or try to move off him. Instead she wrapped her arm around his neck, embracing him.

He was rock hard, but the sight of her flustered turned him on even more, if that was possible. "Soon, I hope you'll be coming around my cock."

Her green eyes widened and in addition to the lust rolling off her, he sensed... not fear exactly, but something that smelled a lot like panic. Another sudden thought hit him. "Do you regret what just happened?"

"No." Her quick answer soothed him. "It's just... this was very unexpected."

"Is that a bad thing?"

Her luscious lips curved up into a small, seductive smile. "Definitely not, but I don't think I'm ready for anything else just yet."

As long as she didn't have any regrets, he could force himself to be patient. Cupping her jaw, he stroked her cheek, enjoying the feel of her. The need to touch her had been overwhelming the past few weeks. Hell, he'd almost lost control earlier when he'd first pulled her onto his lap, and she'd sensed it. "Thank you for calming me down earlier."

"I should be thanking you for..." She trailed off and that delicious color tinged her cheeks again.

"For?" he prompted, wanting to hear her say the words. No, needing. She might be a very sensual woman, but she wasn't a flirt and she didn't flaunt her sexuality. His most primal side wanted her to talk to him in a way she didn't with anyone else. So bad he craved it.

She pursed her lips and slid off his lap. "We should get out of here." A frown marred her face for a moment as she grabbed her purse and pulled her cell phone out of it. "But first I need to call Antoine."

Nikan hadn't even realized he'd growled until Esperanze shot him an annoyed look. "After what just happened I wouldn't think you'd feel threatened by him."

The growl died in his throat. His rational, human side could tell there was no attraction between Esperanze and Antoine. He hadn't scented any sort of lust from the vampire, though the vamp could have been hiding his reaction. Not that it mattered. Esperanze wasn't into anyone but *him*. After tonight he was absolutely certain. Still, his wolf didn't always see reason. Not where his intended mate was concerned.

He watched as she slid her phone back into her purse. "What is it?" he asked.

"He's not answering and before you, uh, interrupted us, he was concerned about something." There was a thread of worry in her voice.

"What about?" He might not like the guy solely for the reason Esperanze used to have a crush on him, but Nikan would help him out to make her happy.

"He didn't say, but would you mind if we stopped by his hotel room before heading back to ours?"

Like he could deny her anything. He shook his head as she began to slide out of the booth. Following, he said, "I thought he lived in DC."

"He does, but he didn't want to deal with traveling to and from the conference so he got a hotel room."

Nikan wrapped an arm around her shoulders, keeping her close. He turned their bodies so that he was in front of her as he pulled the curtain back. He doubted anyone was waiting to jump them, but he wanted to protect her. The crowd had nearly doubled and from the look of things, the night was about to get a lot more hedonistic. Half-dressed paranormal beings and humans writhed on the dance floor, and the men and women he'd seen earlier offering their blood to vamps were apparently also offering other services.

"Oh my," Esperanze breathed out, her voice unsteady.

He looked down to see her face even more flushed than earlier, then tracked her line of sight. Two vampires were sandwiching a female on the dance floor, dancing, groping, and before long he had no doubt they'd be in one of the private booths.

"You like that?" he asked quietly.

She didn't answer, but he scented a trickle of lust rolling off her as she watched, almost entranced. It was an erotic sight and one he appreciated too, but something sharp jumped inside him at the thought of another male touching, or worse, sharing her. "I don't share."

Her head snapped up, her eyes slightly narrowed as she looked at him. "Neither do I." There was a surprising bite to her words he liked.

"Good." As he tightened his grip, she did the same, digging her fingers into his waist with more pressure than before. His entire body tensed at the feel of her pressed up against him. He might have imagined what it would be like to finally have a taste of Esperanze, but nothing had prepared him for the reality. He had no problem being as patient as she needed, but he really hoped she changed her mind about taking things to the next level before this weekend was over. If he could give her so much pleasure she couldn't think straight, it would make it a hell of a lot easier to broach the mating subject.

Chapter 7

Esperanze knocked on Antoine's door, then tried his phone again when he didn't answer.

"He might have hooked up with someone or decided to head back to his home." Nikan stood watch in the hallway of the hotel like he actually was her bodyguard.

It was something she adored about him. No matter what, he was always alert, always ready for any danger, even if it was highly unlikely they'd be facing any. "I know, I just feel bad. He wanted to talk and..." She trailed off, not wanting to bring up what she and Nikan had done less than an hour ago.

Not because she regretted it, but because she wasn't sure where things were headed with them. She didn't have much experience with men and definitely not with alphas. Her lovers had all been betas. Just like her. Things had never been particularly wild or animalistic, just sweet and perfectly pleasurable. And she'd never in a million years thought she'd let someone bring her to orgasm in a public place. Sure, they'd been blocked by a curtain, but that wasn't much of a barrier. Her lower abdomen clenched as she remembered the way Nikan had expertly brought her to release.

It had been exquisite and made her entire body heat up just remembering it.

"Whatever you're thinking about, don't stop." Nikan's voice was low and enticing, bringing her out of her thoughts.

She had to remind herself to control her emotions around him. If she didn't, he'd scent every little change. Now that she'd finally admitted to herself how much she was attracted to him, she kept forgetting to keep herself in check. The past few weeks it had been difficult to hide her desire, but she'd done it. Now he knew exactly how much she craved him and it was impossible to deny it. Sighing, she slid her phone back in her purse. "We can stop by in the morning. He doesn't have a speaking engagement until tomorrow afternoon, but hopefully he'll be back."

Shoving her hands into the pockets of her coat, she started down the hallway with Nikan right next to her. But he didn't give her any space and she wasn't sure if she should be thankful or not. He wrapped an arm around her as they reached the elevator doors and kept that hold all the way out of Antoine's hotel to the one they were staying in next door. Only when they reached their hotel room door did he loosen his grip, and that was only so he could open the door and do a quick search of their room. Since she didn't scent anyone she didn't wait for him to finish his cursory check before stepping inside and closing the door behind her.

Now that they were alone—actually alone with no outside distractions or clubgoers a stone's throw away—panic settled over her skin, feather light. It wasn't a bone deep kind of thing, more like jittery nerves that she couldn't get a handle on.

Trying to ignore his very male presence, she went to her suitcase and pulled out a long-sleeved pajama set. As a shifter she preferred to sleep with a lot less clothing on, but since they were sharing a bed there was no way that was happening. Now she was glad she'd packed pajamas at the last minute. "I'm going to take a shower and get ready for bed," she said as she turned to face him.

Nikan was standing by his own suitcase, which was next to the small breakfast table. For a moment it looked like he might say something, but he just nodded, those dark eyes tracking her every move.

Only once she was behind the closed bathroom door did she allow herself to breathe. Her hands actually shook as she shed her coat and ripped dress. She was thankful for the privacy the small room gave her. Once she was naked, however, she couldn't help but imagining what it would be like to invite Nikan in to join her as she stepped into the shower. She'd seen him in wolf form but never without clothes on, and thoughts of what he'd look like had haunted her fantasies. After pulling her hair into a big clip so it wouldn't get wet, she gritted her teeth and turned the shower knob so that cold water blasted over her. She needed to keep her thoughts tame and her mind off any sort of sex with him. Because thinking about what he would look like naked made all sensible thought fly right out the window.

After a very cold shower, she felt like she had a better grasp on her emotions and was better armed to face Nikan. They were two adults and would have no problem sharing a bed tonight. She could definitely keep her hands to herself. Once she was changed into her pajamas and had brushed her teeth, she scooped up her discarded clothes and opened the door. The room was already dark, but thanks to her extrasensory abilities, it took less than a second for her to adjust.

Before she'd taken two steps Nikan was there, pressing her up against the wall next to the bathroom. His hands cupped her face as his mouth slanted over hers.

She didn't have time to think before his tongue was invading her mouth. He stroked against hers, taking and teasing and sending zings of pleasure to all her nerve endings. She was vaguely aware of her clothes dropping to the floor because she pressed her hands to his chest to steady herself.

That's when it registered he wasn't wearing a shirt. He'd moved so fast she hadn't noticed before, but those were definitely rock hard muscles she was stroking. Allowing herself to roam over the taut planes of his body, she only stopped when he pulled back.

Breathing hard to stare down at her, he said, "I don't care how long you want to wait to... get more physical, but you don't get to pull away from me emotionally."

His words were like ice water slapping her in the face because he read her perfectly. "I wasn't—"

"Yes, you were and I won't let you. After what we just shared, that's not happening. You trusted me enough to let me stroke you to orgasm in a public place. I can't deal with walls right now." He let his hands fall as he took a step back.

When he did, her gaze automatically zeroed in on his chest. She fought to keep her mind from going blank at the gorgeous sight before her. He was completely right. She'd been trying to pull away from him, to put some distance between them for her own sanity. As her eyes drank in what her fingers had just traced, her wolf side tried to tell her human side to get over herself. All those flat planes and sharp striations just begged to be touched. Her hands balled into fists by her sides as she forced herself not to touch him. Sighing she looked back up at him. "Okay, no walls, but if we're sharing a bed tonight, you're wearing a shirt."

He looked almost affronted for a moment before he realized what she meant. What? Had he actually thought she was repulsed by him? She almost snorted at the thought.

"My shirt is staying off," he said as he followed her to the bed.

"No way." She folded her ruined dress and shoved it in her suitcase before pulling the overpacked thing off the bed. Then she pointed to the other side. "You're sleeping on that side *and* you're wearing clothes."

A smile played on his lips as he walked to the other side wearing dark slacks and no shoes. For some reason the sight of his bare feet turned her on too. What was wrong with her? Toes weren't supposed to be sexy. Looking away she grabbed the top of the comforter and pulled down harder than necessary.

He did the same, though not as hard, and didn't make a move to put on a shirt.

She narrowed her eyes at him. "Are you forgetting something?"

"No, and if you push it, these are coming off too." His fingers played with the top button of his pants. "And I'm not wearing any boxers."

Her throat tightened at the last statement, but she found her voice. "Don't even think about it." She slid into the bed and pulled the covers up to her chest. A quick glance at the nightstand reassured her that her cell phone was where she'd placed it earlier. She'd preset her alarm to wake her up in the morning, but she wanted it nearby in case Antoine called.

Turning on her side, she faced Nikan as he slid into bed next to her. Elbow bent, he propped his head up on one hand as he stared at her. Her life would be so much easier if one of them was sleeping on the floor. But she wouldn't ask him to do that and she knew he'd never let her, so it would be pointless to even bring it up. Sharing a bed might be torture, but that was just the way it was.

"I don't think it's fair that you're fully dressed." His voice had dropped a few octaves, taking on an incredibly sensual quality.

Behind Nikan, the curtain to their window was pulled back a few inches, letting some of the unnatural light of other hotels and the city spill into the room. It illuminated his long, lean form. Not that she had any problem seeing him. She almost wished she couldn't see him so well. "Life isn't fair," she said quietly, holding back a grin at his soft growl. He scooted a few inches closer so she took one of the pillows and placed it in between them. "No way. You stay on your side." If he touched her right now, it would short-circuit her ability to reason.

Completely ignoring her, he tossed the pillow to the floor then tugged her close to him. Wrapping his arms around her, he pulled her until her head was on his chest and she was practically draped around him. Esperanze thought about pulling away, but deep down, she didn't want to.

He wasn't being sexual, just holding her close. Even though she could feel his erection pressing against her abdomen thanks to their intertwined position, he was simply stroking down her back with his hand in a gentle rhythmic motion.

She sighed and relaxed more into him. "I'm glad you came with me to the conference. Alicia's death hit me and my sisters pretty hard. Then to lose Carmen… I don't know how Ana is keeping it together so well." Ana was one of her older cousins, their Alpha's bondmate, and she'd recently lost a sister too. They'd all lost packmates a couple months ago due to a rapid, vicious poisoning of their pack, but it had happened so fast and they'd all had one another to lean on. To lose two of their youngest, sweetest members so recently had been a brutal blow to the entire pack, reminding them they could still be targeted by blind, ignorant fools.

His grip around her tightened. "I would have come even without Connor's approval."

Those quiet words whispered against the top of her head made her pause. He was basically saying he would have defied his Alpha to come with her. But that couldn't be right, could it? Afraid to ask him if that was truly what he meant—and afraid of how she'd feel if he said yes—she closed her eyes and allowed herself to savor the feel of Nikan's strong embrace.

Tomorrow she could worry about their future. Tonight she just wanted to sleep knowing she was utterly safe and protected in the arms of a man she was falling for more and more each second that passed.

Chapter 8

Nikan gave Esperanze another covert look as they headed down the hallway toward Antoine's room. She'd called her friend this morning and he'd told her to forget about their conversation last night. Nikan had been able to hear the phone call and it was obvious the vampire sounded anxious.

And that had stressed Esperanze out. Whatever her feelings were for Antoine, they weren't remotely sexual and Nikan hated seeing her distressed. So, they were on their way to see her former professor whether he wanted to see them or not.

Esperanze was wearing dark, slim-fitting jeans, black knee-high boots and a snug black wraparound sweater that accentuated all her curves. She might be petite, but damn she was curvy and soft in all the right places. Just like a woman—his woman—should be. She'd loosely braided her hair, letting it fall down her back, and all he could think about was freeing it and running his hands through it as she rode him.

Patience.

He might not be a pro at the whole patience thing, but he'd do any damn thing she wanted. Holding her last night against him had been just as good as sex—*almost*. Feeling all those curves and hearing her softly breathing against his chest had been fucking heaven. He loved that she'd trusted him enough to let him hold her all night. He had been afraid for a brief moment when he'd tugged her close that she'd resist. But she hadn't.

He'd known her long enough that he realized her trust didn't come easy. Though she looked to be in her early twenties, at eighty she was the same age as him, and before he and the rest of Connor's warriors had united their packs she'd been sheltered. He'd heard enough about her old Alpha that he knew the guy hadn't trusted humans or outsiders. Not to mention that Esperanze hadn't been very friendly with any of the other warriors except him. He'd pretty much made it impossible for her to ignore him—showing up at her house for dinners, escorting her everywhere around the ranch, helping her out with the little ones—and she'd been wary at first. But after a few days she'd relaxed. Still, letting her guard down enough to share a bed with him, trusting him not to make a move—it touched him.

Even so, it bugged him that she hadn't responded to him saying that he would have defied their Alpha for her, but there wasn't much he could do about it. Hell, he had some pride left. He'd all but admitted his feelings for her and she hadn't said anything. He wasn't going to demand she respond. And that had nothing to do with pride. If she didn't feel the same way—damn, he didn't even want to go there.

As they neared the door to Antoine's room, Nikan put his arm out to stop Esperanze from going any further as he jerked to a halt. His canines ached as the sudden scent of blood permeated the air.

There were a lot of various scents in the hotel—shifters of all varieties, vamps, demons, humans—but the groaning coming from the room they were headed to didn't sound pleasurable. Mixed with the distinctive coppery scent of blood, he knew something was off.

"Is that Antoine?" Esperanze whispered, frozen in place.

Nikan put one finger to his lips then motioned for her to move back. He wanted to tell her to leave the hotel completely, or at least go down to the lobby, but knew she'd argue and didn't want to waste time.

Nodding, she took a couple steps back and pressed her back up against the wall. He stepped partially to the side as he knocked on the door.

Inside there was a hushing sound then another thump, which sounded like someone being punched if the muffled groan was any indication. When no one answered, he knocked again. "Antoine, I know you're in there. Don't make me bust the door open." Nikan didn't plan to, but he scented more than just Antoine inside, and someone was hurt, he was almost sure of it.

A second later the door flew open and a shifter with buzz-cut dark hair and olive-toned skin answered the door. The scent of blood intensified. It wasn't overwhelming, but Nikan scented it just the same.

"Who the fuck are you?" The shifter was an alpha without a doubt, but he was no warrior.

Nikan quickly scanned the guy, taking in the leather jacket, ripped jeans, shit-kickers, silver ring with a wolf emblem on his right hand... and his bloodied fists. He was young, maybe no more than thirty. "Where's Antoine?"

Dark eyes flashed with annoyance. "I asked you a question."

Reaching out, Nikan grabbed the guy by the neck and lifted him off the ground. The lupine shifter struck out with a fist, but Nikan seized him by the wrist, released his neck and whipped him around, shoving him against the open door before he could defend himself. Holding him by the back of the neck, Nikan slammed the alpha's face into the door.

Bone crunched as the door cracked under the impact. The guy let out a brief scream before Nikan slammed his head against the door again. Then he passed out. Blood spurted everywhere, dripping down the door, staining the plush carpet.

The action was violent and brutal, but Nikan scented someone else inside and he'd needed to take this guy out first. He couldn't be distracted or risk being taken on by more than one unknown threat. Not with Esperanze so close.

"What the—" Out of the corner of his eye Nikan watched as another man rounded the corner of the room.

Hating to leave Esperanze exposed for even a second, Nikan knew he had no choice but to venture farther inside. Turning toward the other male who looked almost exactly like the shifter he'd just knocked out, Nikan ducked as the guy threw a punch.

It was a solid throw, but Nikan was older and a hell of a lot faster. As he dodged to the side, he came back up with a fist of his own. Connecting with the guy's jaw, he didn't use all his force. He wanted one of these guys conscious.

The guy's head snapped back and he stumbled but didn't lose his footing. "Who the hell are you?" he snarled.

Nikan quickly scanned the room. Antoine sat on the bed staring at him, his face covered in blood and bruises, though he was already healing. A chair was turned over and the covers were slightly messed up, but there wasn't damage to the room otherwise.

Keeping the majority of his focus on the shifter, Nikan launched himself at the guy. He punched him in the stomach this time. As the guy groaned and swung out, Nikan grabbed his arm, wrenched it back and slammed him face first onto the bed.

Antoine jumped up and gave him space. Before Nikan could start questioning the shifter he scented Esperanze getting closer.

Damn it!

"What happened? What did they do to you?" Her panicked voice rolled over him as she moved into the room, hurrying to Antoine's side.

The shifter Nikan had pinned wasn't struggling, but he was tense, no doubt waiting to make a move if he found an opening. Nikan tightened the grip he had on the back of his neck.

"I owe these guys some money. They were here collecting, that's all. Just let him go. This is my fault," Antoine said quickly, but there wasn't much conviction in his voice.

"Is that right?" Nikan leaned down and growled in the guy's ear.

"Yeah, now fucking let me go," the dark-haired shifter snapped.

"Who's your Alpha?"

"No one! I don't answer to anyone and I'm not doing anything wrong. This vamp can't pay up so me and my brother roughed him up."

Without responding, Nikan reached into the guy's back pocket and pulled out his wallet. He tossed it to Esperanze who caught it with a squeak of surprise. "Will you memorize his ID?"

She flipped open the brown leather wallet. After a few seconds she nodded again then gave it back to him.

"I'm going to let you up, but if you make one wrong move, I won't give you a warning. I'll just kill you." With Esperanze so close, Nikan was barely restraining his inner wolf from taking over and attacking this unknown threat.

"All right," the guy said.

As soon as Nikan let him up, he jumped over the bed, putting distance between himself and the three of them. That was fine with Nikan. He wanted this guy as far away from Esperanze as possible. It was taking all his control not to shift to his wolf form.

"You're gonna pay for this," the guy said to Antoine.

Behind him, the vampire was silent, but Nikan didn't take his eyes off the shifter.

"If I see you in this hotel again, you'll regret it. And I'll be reporting you to the Council." He probably wouldn't but wanted to scare the guy.

The shifter shrugged as his gaze moved back to Nikan. "You think they're gonna give a shit about some money issues we're having with a fucking vampire?"

Unfortunately the guy was probably right. "They will if this screws up shifter-vamp relations."

Another shrug. "He's not protected by anyone."

Damn. If a vampire didn't belong to a coven they had no one to look after them. Vamps tended to congregate together, but there were a lot that chose to live alone, more so than shifters. Sure, the Brethren, the small group of four ancient vamps that ruled all vampires, would intervene if there were serious issues going on between the different species, but for the most part vamps governed themselves. It took a lot for their leaders to get involved with the everyday lives of their people. Nikan's own Council was almost as bad, but not quite. "Get out of here before I change my mind and do to you what I did to your brother."

The guy looked at Antoine again, snarled, then left, hefting his brother up as he backtracked from the room. Once they were gone Nikan shut the cracked door then hurried to Esperanze's side. The need to touch her was overwhelming and the only way to convince his inner wolf she was safe. Barely keeping his wolf chained, he ran his knuckles down her cheek, savoring her softness, before turning to Antoine. "What's really going on?"

"I told you, I owe those guys money."

Nikan shook his head, annoyance popping inside him. "Your lies have a metallic scent to them."

Antoine was silent until Esperanze moved closer to him. She grasped the vamp's hands in her much smaller ones, making Nikan's wolf claw at his insides, shredding and tearing, eager to add to the blood on Antoine's face. Damn, this need to mate was making him crazy.

"Tell us what's going on. Trust Nikan, he'll help you if he can. We both will," Esperanze said softly.

Her words were like a soothing balm over Nikan. Still, he hated the sight of her touching another male. Any male, regardless of species. He balled his hands into fists. No need to act like a complete fucking Neanderthal and piss Essie off.

"I..." Antoine withdrew his hands from Esperanze and scrubbed them over his face. "Fuck! I'll just say it. They took Chandra and they're using her to get to me."

Nikan had heard enough. He pointed to the bed. "Sit." It looked as if the vamp was close to breaking down and Nikan wanted answers that made sense. After Antoine did as he ordered, he continued. "Who is Chandra? And what do they want you for?"

"She's my... well, we're not involved, *yet*. She's a human friend of mine. A biology professor at the college." He looked at Esperanze, a ghost of a smile on his drawn, pale face. "You'd like her, Esperanze." Shaking his head, he refocused on Nikan. "I'd planned to ask her to undergo the change so we could be together always, but something happened. I don't know how they knew she meant something to me. Maybe they were watching, I don't know..." He scrubbed another hand over his face.

"Who was watching?" Nikan demanded. He didn't have time for kid gloves.

Antoine's head tilted toward the door. "Gregorio and Marco Moretti, those two young shifters. They're blackmailing me."

"For what?" Esperanze asked.

He looked at Nikan, his face distraught. "If I tell you, I don't care what you do to me, but you have to swear you'll help save my friend."

Nikan shook his head. "I'm not swearing to anything until you tell me exactly what's going on."

The vampire pursed his lips and stood. "Then leave."

Esperanze swiveled to Nikan, placing a hand on his forearm. She gently squeezed. "Nikan."

Damn, I am so screwed. All she had to do was use that pleading voice and he'd say yes to almost anything. He looked sharply at Antoine. "Fine. I'll help your female."

"Swear it."

"If he says he will, that's good enough," Esperanze interjected, heat in her voice.

Nikan's chest swelled with pride. She might not return his feelings with the same intensity as him, but she trusted him and that meant a hell of a lot. To have the trust of a woman like Esperanze... he swallowed back a lump of foreign emotion.

Antoine nodded. "They've been holding her hostage in exchange for my blood. They're selling it."

The space grew deathly quiet. Nikan couldn't even hear sounds from the neighboring rooms. Selling any paranormal blood was illegal in every circle. Human, shifter, fae, demon and especially vampire. Vampire blood gave humans supernatural strength, giving them power and a euphoric rush, making them reckless, dangerous to everyone. But Nikan pushed past it. That was a problem they'd deal with later. Now, his only interest was helping the innocent human involved. "Why did they take your woman? Why not just take you instead?"

He laughed wryly. "I only wish they had, but I'm too high profile. While I'm not part of a coven, I'm still very well known in many academic circles. If I disappeared, someone would come looking."

"Why not go to the Brethren? I don't really know much about vampires, but wouldn't they help?" Esperanze asked, confusion in her voice.

Nikan snorted softly, already knowing the answer. She obviously didn't understand their hierarchy.

Antoine shook his head. "They'd have done nothing if I'd gone to them for help over a mere human. If she'd been turned, they might have intervened, especially since it's shifters that have her. Now I can't go to them."

"Why?" she persisted.

"I've been giving shifters my blood. They'd kill me for that alone and Chandra would be dead. And in case you're wondering, I briefly thought about going to the cops but the humans already know she's missing. They've even questioned me about her since we work together. The Moretti brothers threatened to kill her if I spoke to the authorities again and they'll do it. I have no one to turn to."

"Have you tried tracking them to see where she's being held?" Nikan asked.

Antoine nodded. "Over the past few weeks I've tried a couple times. They've been very careful each time they come to see me."

"How often is that?"

"Three times a week."

Nikan frowned. "Why did they rough you up this morning? You're their cash cow. It doesn't make sense."

The vampire rubbed a hand over his ribs, as if in pain. "I demanded to talk to her. They haven't let me talk to her in a week and I told them if they didn't let me today, I was walking away.

I... wouldn't have, but I've been going crazy thinking about her. Last time we spoke she was in good spirits and it didn't sound as if they'd hurt her, but these two are animals. I can only imagine what they're capable of. This morning they stopped by to 're-mind' me who was in charge."

Nikan reached out and tugged Esperanze close. This weekend was supposed to have been about her seduction and pleasure. He'd even planned to stay a few extra days, spend more time with her, maybe do some touristy sightseeing stuff. Dealing with rogue shifters selling vamp blood? Something he'd never imagined. He wanted to pack Esperanze up and get the hell out of town. Keeping her out of danger was his number one priority, but she'd hate him if he did. And the truth was, he'd hate himself if he walked away from helping an innocent human.

"We've got to help him." Esperanze wrapped her arm around his waist, curling into him as she nuzzled her head against his chest.

"I know." His fingers tightened on her shoulder as he looked at Antoine. "I want to know every single thing you know about these two shifters. Everything you've noticed no matter how small." He turned to Esperanze, his voice automatically softening. "And I need to know the info you memorized from that ID."

"That was Gregorio," Antoine said.

Esperanze nodded in agreement. "That's what it said on his license."

Names might not be much, but at least they were a start. Before joining with the Armstrong pack, Nikan had lived on his mother's reservation. For decades, the elders of his Potawatomi tribe had come to him to settle disputes because of his shifter ability to scent lies. He'd also been called upon by local law enforcement for help in tracking lost kids or missing persons once paranormal beings had come out to the rest of the world. He might not like the idea of staying in DC, but he liked the thought of helping out an innocent.

Chapter 9

Esperanze sat on the edge of the big bed in her and Nikan's hotel room. Antoine sat at the small breakfast table, his head in his hands. He might have changed out of his bloody clothes and completely healed from the bruises and lacerations, but he still looked awful.

Seeing him so torn up broke her heart, especially since she understood his worry. The thought of losing a man she cared about—namely Nikan—shredded her insides. She'd put herself in Antoine's shoes earlier as he'd told them why he was giving up his blood, and she couldn't find any room in her heart for judgment. If someone took Nikan, she'd do anything to keep him safe.

The realization had slammed into her with startling force. She might want to deny how much she cared for him, but it was becoming impossible. Considering how he'd stepped up and was helping Antoine with no concern for his own safety made her feelings for him swell even more.

Antoine had cancelled his speaking engagements today and she wouldn't be going to anything else either. Nothing mattered now except helping his friend.

She nearly jumped when the hotel room door opened, but her heart rate steadied when Nikan stepped inside. They'd been very careful after leaving Antoine's hotel, but Nikan still wanted to make sure they hadn't been followed.

"We're clear." He pulled out his cell phone as he spoke. She knew who he was calling before their Alpha even picked up.

"Hey, man. How's the conference? You and Esperanze mated yet?" Thanks to her extrasensory abilities she could hear Connor's questions clearly.

Hearing that question made her heart stutter and her breath catch. Nikan stared at her, his expression completely unreadable. She held her breath as she waited for him to answer.

"We've run into a big problem." Nikan's voice was rock steady.

Something that felt a lot like disappointment surged through her when Nikan didn't even touch what Connor had asked. Intellectually, she knew it wasn't the time or place to even care about his nonresponsiveness, but it stung in a way she didn't completely understand. Mating with an alpha wasn't something she'd ever planned on. Of course she'd never planned to fall for a warrior like Nikan either.

Silently, she waited as Nikan outlined to their Alpha everything that had just happened. Nikan also gave him all the information they had on the two shifters' identities to pass on to Ryan, their resident computer genius/hacker at the ranch. Finally her Alpha spoke and her spirits plummeted. "I can't spare the manpower right now. Not with everything going on at the ranch. Everyone's still healing from Alicia and Carmen's deaths and there are still members of the Antiparanormal League who want us dead. I only let you go because—"

Nikan cut him off, his dark gaze never wavering from hers. "I know why and I appreciate it."

Fighting the urge to look away, Esperanze stood, ready to grab the phone and plead with her Alpha for more manpower, but Connor continued. "But I might know someone in the area who can help. I'm going to make a call, but in the meantime I'll let Ryan know about this, so be waiting for a text or e-mail from him. Sit tight and give me half an hour."

"Will do. Thanks." Nikan slid his phone in his pocket after they disconnected.

Antoine, who had been silent, finally let out a small groan. "Your Alpha isn't going to help us. Why would he help a vampire?" Anger laced each word.

"Because he cares about our pack," Esperanze snapped, angry at her friend's depressing attitude. "I'm sorry your friend is being held captive, but I just lost my sister and cousin. Before that half my pack was wiped out from poisoning so stop feeling sorry for yourself! You're not doing Chandra or yourself any favors by acting this way. That's pathetic and it's time for you to man up." She felt bad for her harsh words, but he needed to snap out of his pity party or they'd never accomplish anything. Right now it wasn't about him. It was about an innocent woman being held captive.

Antoine stared at her for a long moment, his blue eyes unblinking. The temperature in the room felt as if it dropped a few degrees with the icy stare he gave her. He stood suddenly, and behind her she felt Nikan move closer. His arm snaked around her waist as he pulled her close so that her back pressed against his chest.

"Excuse me for a moment." Antoine's voice was monotone as he strode toward the bathroom.

Instead of turning around she laid her head back against Nikan's chest, drawing on his raw strength and warmth. "Was I too harsh?" she whispered even though it was likely Antoine could hear her over the water she heard from the bathroom.

Nikan shook his head, his chin moving over the top of her head. "No, someone needed to say it. It's better that it came from you. Now we just wait for Connor's call."

Esperanze hated the thought of just waiting, but there wasn't much of a choice. Unfortunately it would give her time to think about what she'd just heard. There was only one reason Connor would have asked if they were mated yet. Nikan had talked to their Alpha about her and it wasn't something he'd do lightly.

She wasn't sure how she felt about Nikan asking to take her as his mate. Part of her wished she could pretend this was sudden, but deep down the most primal part of her had acknowledged Nikan's interest in her a while ago—and the fact that she reciprocated. As soon as he and the rest of Connor's warriors had arrived at the ranch he'd been around her every single day without fail. She'd gotten to the point where she couldn't imagine not seeing him each day. Her wolf wanted to dance every time he was near.

And after what they'd shared last night she knew she wanted more from him. Not just physically, though that was something she was looking forward to. No, she enjoyed his quiet company.

If he didn't have anything to say, he never tried to fill silences, and she appreciated that. Not that they had much silence between them. She'd learned practically everything about his past in the first week they started hanging out. He'd seemed almost surprised with himself when he'd opened up to her, but it hadn't taken long for her to warm up to him either. It was almost like her wolf recognized him and trusted him. He had so much character too. If he didn't, he wouldn't be helping out a vampire who meant nothing to him. Nikan might be doing this because of her, but he was also doing it because of the innocent human woman involved. Of that, she had no doubt.

Still, old fears and insecurities bubbled up inside Esperanze, bitter and angry. While Nikan was nothing like her father who had insisted on controlling everything about her mother's life, he was still an alpha, a warrior, and he was stronger than she was. Shifter rules and human rules were different. In her world, the strongest governed, and if she allowed him into every facet of her life she'd be putting herself at risk to submit to him. What if he expected some perfect, submissive little beta that she could never be? Her father had expected that from her mother and while he hadn't been physically abusive, he'd been ridiculously possessive to the point that he'd almost snuffed out her mother's natural zest for life. She'd slowly become a quieter, more reserved woman, so different from how she'd been when Esperanze was a young pup.

"Why did Connor ask if we were mated yet?" *No! Why did I ask that?* Esperanze wanted to kick herself. The question had slipped out as too many questions and worries raced through her head. She hadn't been able to control herself.

Nikan's grip tightened around her, his embrace like steel bands, and his earthy scent seemed to intensify as he leaned down. His mouth brushed her ear, sending a delicious shiver rolling through her. "Are you sure you're ready for the answer?"

Chapter 10

The feel of Esperanze's back against his chest, her petite body curved into him, was so perfect. His canines ached, demanding to lengthen, to sink into the soft flesh of Esperanze's neck and leave a permanent mark as he pushed deep inside her.

But he wasn't a complete fucking animal. He couldn't and wouldn't just take from her. Wouldn't demand more than she was ready for. Right now she held all the cards. She completely owned him even if she didn't realize it. No other female made him want the things she did: a permanent home, kids, a woman to wake up to every morning. But not just any woman. It had to be Esperanze. She was so sweet and giving, taking care of her sisters and keeping them positive after Alicia's death. Some alphas might look at betas as weak, but he knew differently. They might be physically weaker but they were the backbone of any pack. Esperanze was the perfect example with her inner strength.

He was practically holding his breath as he waited for her response. If she was ready for the answer, he'd tell her exactly why Connor asked and exactly what he wanted from her. Which was pretty much everything.

As Esperanze started to turn in his arms, the bathroom door flew open. Antoine flew out, his eyes wide as he held out his phone.

"They're calling," he whispered, as if the shifters on the other end could hear.

Nikan gritted his teeth, resenting the interruption, but he also hated that they were making contact before he'd spoken to Connor again. Releasing Esperanze from his hold, he grabbed a pen and small pad of paper with the hotel's logo on it from the breakfast table in case he needed to write down instructions. He nodded at Antoine. "Answer it."

Swallowing hard, the vampire did as he said. "Hello?"

"Who the hell were those two shifters this morning?" Nikan recognized the voice as Gregorio, the one he'd spoken to.

Conference, Nikan mouthed.

"They're colleagues from the conference. We were supposed to meet for drinks last night and I didn't show up so they were worried." Antoine's voice only shook a fraction.

Nikan was impressed by how well he was keeping it together compared to the way he'd been moaning only minutes before.

"So you're friends with shifters now?" A snide question.

"I'm friends with all species." Antoine's answer was immediate.

Thank God, Nikan thought. The vamp needed to keep his cool for his kidnapped friend's sake.

"Are they going to make trouble?"

"No. I convinced them I just owe you money. They even offered to give me some."

Gregorio laughed, the harsh sound streaming clearly through the phone line. "That's fucking rich. If you're lying, Chandra will pay."

"I'm not lying," Antoine said.

There was a brief silence, but Gregorio finally spoke again. "We need you tonight for a special client. He wants his product directly from the source."

Nikan shook his head and mouthed no.

Antoine faltered, but nodded. "I'm not letting someone drink from me."

"You'll do exactly what we say... but he doesn't want to drink *from* you. He just wants to make sure what he's getting is the real deal. Wants to see exactly where the blood is coming from."

Nikan scribbled on the note pad. *You want to see Chandra first.*

Antoine nodded as he spoke into the phone. "I want to see Chandra, know that she's okay first."

He laughed again. "No fucking way, but I'll let you talk to her."

There was a brief rustling in the background; then a female voice came over the line. "Antoine?"

"Chandra," he breathed out on a sigh of relief. "Are you hurt?"

"No, I... I'm fine, but... I'm s-scared, Antoine." Her words were slow and measured as if she was trying hard to get them out. "How long..." She trailed off, and Nikan heard Gregorio in the background telling her to shut up.

"I'm so sorry, Chandra. I'm doing everything they say. I'll get you—"

Nikan shook his head sharply. He didn't want the vamp making any sort of promises to save her. The brothers didn't need to be suspicious that there was a plan in the works to help her.

Antoine swallowed hard again and nodded. "Just promise me you're not hurt."

"I promise." She slurred the 's' as she spoke. "I can't tell you more, but I promise I'm okay. I... miss you."

Antoine closed his eyes and his jaw clenched once. "I miss you too." His voice was ragged.

Nikan felt a rush of pity for the guy. If anything happened to Esperanze, he'd go insane. And anyone who got in his way... his wolf flexed its claws, not wanting to travel down that path. Esperanze was anxiously sitting on the edge of the bed, safe in this hotel room with him. He was going to keep it that way.

Gregorio came back on the line. "See? We're taking care of your female. Now listen carefully." The rogue shifter outlined instructions to where Antoine would be going in a couple hours then disconnected after a threat not to tell anyone or else.

"Does he call from the same number every time?" Nikan asked the moment they disconnected.

Antoine shook his head. "No, it's a new one each time. I have an acquaintance I trust enough not to repeat my request, and I asked him to trace a couple of the numbers. All burner phones. They must toss them after each time they call me. I have no way of contacting them because they always call me."

Nikan inwardly cursed. It had been a small shot. A possible way for his packmate Ryan to track these guys down. His phone buzzed once indicating a message, and when he glanced at the ID, he gave a wry smile. Ryan.

As he opened the message, Esperanze sidled up next to him. "Is it important?"

"Maybe..." He scrolled through Ryan's brief message outlining the lives of the Moretti brothers, holding the phone out so Esperanze could read too.

Ryan's text told them that the brothers were packless, parents likely killed by vampires five years ago according to a cold case file. The address on their licenses was bogus, listing an abandoned warehouse, but he hadn't had time to run their financials. Not much, but Nikan knew Ryan would come through if there was any information to be found. As he finished the message, his phone rang. "Yeah?"

"Found someone to help you guys. Name's Thabit, he's a feline—jaguar shifter," Connor said.

"He doesn't mind helping out a couple of lupines and a vamp?" Nikan didn't give a shit about species differences. His mother had been human, had been turned into a shifter because of her pregnancy with him, and his father was a white shifter. He might have grown up on a reservation, but he'd grown up in a time where racism and prejudice had been more prevalent.

"Not at all. He's on his way to your hotel room. Said he's at your disposal."

"How long until he gets here?"

"Half an hour, maybe less. He doesn't live there but he's in the area. When I told him about the human he had no problem helping."

Nikan raised his eyebrows. Not all supernatural beings cared about humans. At least not to the extent they'd volunteer to help out strangers. "Thanks."

Connor grunted. "Just keep me updated. If things get too fucked up, you pull out and call me. The pack can't afford to lose anyone right now. *I* can't afford to lose you."

"I will." Nikan slid his phone into his pocket, thankful for an Alpha like Connor. When the tall Scottish shifter had approached him about starting his own pack, a pack made entirely of warriors, he'd been hesitant at first. But his inner wolf had needed that connection and he'd bled alongside Connor. They all had. Now more than ever he was grateful he'd made the decision to join with the Alpha since it had led him to Esperanze.

"Now what?" she asked, her voice tearing him out of his thoughts.

"Now we figure out how to save Antoine's friend." No matter how much he wanted to finish the conversation they'd started barely ten minutes before, it would have to wait.

Chapter 11

Watching Nikan's hard expression, Esperanze felt as if her skin was too tight for her body. She'd been about to spill all her fears and worries to Nikan when Antoine's call had interrupted them. Now the three of them were just waiting for Connor's contact to show up. The room was thick with tension. Sexual for her and Nikan. Antoine was nervous and tense and couldn't stop pacing around the room.

Since he was supposed to meet the pair of rogue shifters in less than two hours she didn't blame him.

When Nikan suddenly tensed, she glanced over to find him staring at the door. His entire body had gone rigid. A moment later there was a knock on the door. He covered the distance to it before she'd blinked.

As he cautiously opened it, she scented a feline shifter. Of all the various shifters, felines were the easiest for her to scent other than lupine. A man the same height as Nikan stepped into the room. With smooth coffee colored skin, eerie blue eyes that seemed to almost glow against his dark face and sharp, defined cheeks, the shifter was *very* good looking. Almost too good looking. If it wasn't for the very apparent edge of danger that seemed to surround him like a shroud, his features could almost be defined as feminine.

"I'm Thabit. Connor said you would be expecting me," he said to Nikan, his voice much deeper than expected.

Nikan nodded and moved back, letting him enter the room. "I'm Nikan, this is Esperanze and that is Antoine." He nodded at the vampire pacing by the open window.

Antoine stopped and grunted a hello to him. Refraining from snapping at her former professor, Esperanze smiled and strode toward Thabit. "Thank you for helping us. Antoine is grateful too, he's just worried about his friend." She held out a hand to the newcomer.

"It's a pleasure to meet you. Connor said nothing of your beauty." He held her hand much longer than necessary, lightly stroking her palm with his thumb. His eyes were directly on hers and he wasn't looking at her too inappropriately, but the forward action took her so off guard she could only stare at him.

Nikan growled low in his throat, instantly moving between them, tugging her close to his side. His tight grip around her hip was proprietary, and she knew the only reason he was showing control was because Connor had sent the other shifter. Otherwise, he'd have likely unsheathed his claws. "Esperanze is taken."

Those vivid blue eyes flicked to Nikan. He shrugged, obviously not apologetic. "You haven't marked her."

"*Yet.*" The word tore from Nikan's throat, the sound more animal than human.

Oh, crap. She couldn't dwell on the word "yet" right now because she didn't know if that was something he'd just said to get this guy to back off or if he actually meant it. Last night he'd been territorial in the club, so much so that she'd needed to calm him down. They so didn't have time for that right now. Leaning into his embrace, she placed a palm over his chest. "Before you two start measuring your dicks, we have more important things to worry about. The Moretti brothers want to meet Antoine in about an hour and a half and he'll need a solid thirty minutes to get there. We need to figure out what we're going to do."

Thabit looked over at Antoine, his lips pulling into a thin line. "I've never met a daywalker before."

Antoine didn't move from the window, his expression drawn and haggard as he stared at Thabit. Esperanze wanted to shake him out of his pity party. He had three people willing to help him and he was acting defeated. "Well, now you have," he said drily. "I've already told Esperanze and Nikan that they want to meet me at an abandoned warehouse. We've met there before. There isn't much life around there except for the homeless, which makes it easier for them to control the environment. From there, they blindfold me, drive me somewhere and draw my blood. This time it seems they have different plans."

Raw energy practically pulsed off Nikan as he not so subtly moved to keep himself between her and Thabit. "We're going to follow you this time. You said you've never met anyone else in their operation so if it's just the two of them, we should be able track them back to where they're keeping Chandra."

"But what if they don't go back to her today? Or what if they see you and decide to hurt her?"

Esperanze gritted her teeth. His questions were valid, but this was a completely different side to Antoine. He'd always seemed so sophisticated and put together. It hadn't surprised her that a vampire had offered to turn him. Looking at him now, she realized no amount of polish, money or education could give him what Nikan had in spades. Confidence, control and an innate strength. Granted it wasn't Nikan's friend's life on the line, but he always kept his cool.

Before she could say anything, Nikan spoke. "Anything could go wrong, Antoine. If you don't want our help, we'll walk away. Then you're not risking anything. You also won't be helping the woman you claim to care so much for."

The three of them stood there, watching until finally he nodded. "You're right and... I'm sorry. I appreciate your help. I've just never felt so fucking helpless in my life."

Thabit cleared his throat, drawing their attention to him. "We can't follow in one vehicle. It will give them too many opportunities to see us. One of us will follow for a while, then inform the other via cell phone where we're turning off. Then the other can pick up the tail."

Nikan nodded. "I agree. After our run-in with them this morning, they'll be more careful. Esperanze and I will ride in one car and you can ride in yours. Did you drive here?"

The feline shifter nodded.

"Good. We'll leave now that we have the address. It can't hurt to get there early. Antoine, can you make it back to your hotel's parking garage unseen?"

He nodded. "I'll be invisible."

Once he'd left, Nikan and Thabit exchanged phone numbers so they'd have a way to contact each other if they got separated. Esperanze knew without asking that the only reason Nikan was trusting this other shifter so much was because he had their Alpha's backing. Connor never would have sent someone he wouldn't have trusted to watch his own back.

As they rode the elevator down to the parking garage below the lobby level, Esperanze shot Nikan a quick look. "Before we arrived in DC, I memorized the grid pattern of all the roads. And all the traffic laws. Did you know some streets become one way after a certain time of day?"

His eyebrows drew together. "No."

"Well they do and the streets can be very confusing from what I've read." She didn't have an eidetic memory exactly, but pretty close. Before she'd realized Nikan was coming with her she'd memorized the layout of the city because she always liked to be prepared.

"It's true," Thabit said, his deep voice echoing around the enclosed space. "I hate driving in this city."

Nikan briefly glanced at the other male then looked back at her and nodded politely, as if he was unsure why she was telling him. "Okay."

"I want to drive," she said as the elevator dinged and the doors whooshed open.

Now his eyebrows shot up. "What?"

"It'll be easier if I drive. When we're following Antoine there will be periods of time when we won't see the vehicle and since we won't know where they're taking him we can't use the navigator. This way I won't have to shout out instructions if we get turned around. It will make things smoother."

Thabit palmed a set of keys. "I'll let you two figure this out and meet you at the entrance. I'm driving a black four-door sedan. Low key, shouldn't draw attention."

Nikan didn't even glance at Thabit as he left, but kept his focus entirely on her. He gave her this look like he was trying to figure something out. Then he tossed her his keys. "If there's any damage, you're paying me back for the deposit." The slight note of humor and his quick acquiescence took her off guard.

It also pleased her since she'd expected resistance. As an alpha warrior, he'd just let her know how much he valued her without saying a word. By letting her be in control of this situation, he'd made it clear that her beta status didn't matter in his eyes. They were equals. Something warm blossomed in her chest, spreading throughout her entire body. Nikan was different from any alpha she'd ever known. Different from any man she'd ever known. She planned to tell him just that very soon.

As they headed for the rental, her boots clicked against the pavement. Turning, she started to respond when he gave her a look so hungry and lustful it took her off guard.

"Don't think I've forgotten our conversation. No matter what happens with Antoine today, we *will* finish it." His dark eyes flashed a shade darker and she knew it wasn't a trick of the light.

Unable to find her voice, she nodded. She had no doubt they'd finish the conversation. Given what she had to say, things between them would change forever.

Chapter 12

Nikan crouched low, peering down from the roof of the run-down two-story building he and Esperanze were on. Neglected duplexes and empty warehouses dotted the industrial area where crime had left its mark. The farther into this northeast neighborhood they'd driven, the more working girls and drug deals they'd seen—in broad daylight.

The abandoned building with boarded up windows and graffiti tags they were using as their lookout was thankfully uninhabited. He and Esperanze had decided to park beside it once they realized they were close to Antoine's meeting place.

Thabit had chosen the building next to theirs so they weren't all clustered together. Nikan had his hands-free earpiece in so they were able to easily communicate. He might not have liked the way the guy eyed Esperanze, but Connor had sent him. After they saved Antoine's woman, he didn't plan to stick around and grab a beer with the guy. He intended to get Esperanze alone as soon as possible so they could figure out what was going on between the two of them.

Across the street behind a dilapidated chain link fence with huge chunks cut out of it, a flashy black Mercedes had been idling for the past ten minutes in front of a ramshackle warehouse. Though they couldn't see past the tinted windows, Nikan was sure the Moretti brothers were inside since it was the scheduled meet place. And they'd been early.

"I see him," Esperanze whispered next to Nikan. Crouching down in the same position as him, her leg was lined up against his as she peered over the building. She passed him the binoculars Thabit had let them borrow.

He could see well without them, but took them anyway. Antoine was pulling up in his gray Land Rover. As he stepped out of the vehicle, he started to glance around, then caught himself. Nikan only hoped whoever was inside the car hadn't noticed.

A moment later, the driver and passenger door opened and the two men from earlier stepped out. Before they'd even spoke to each other, Marco, the one Nikan had knocked out, punched Antoine in the stomach, then in the face.

Esperanze let out a hiss and Nikan instinctively rested a hand on her knee. Energy hummed through her, but she didn't make a move. There was nothing any of them could do.

"They're probably still angry at him for our appearance this morning and they might be testing to see if he brought backup," he said.

Her mouth was a grim line. "I know, but I hate seeing him get beat up."

"He'll heal," Nikan said softly, knowing it wouldn't make a difference to Esperanze. With each punch, she tensed underneath his fingers.

After a few minutes, they stopped abusing him and practically dragged him to the car. They shoved him into the back. Then Marco slid into the front seat of Antoine's Land Rover while Gregorio got back in their own vehicle.

His packmate Ryan had sent what he could dig up on their financials on the drive over and it looked like for the last six months the two brothers had been making sizable deposits into a couple offshore accounts. Since Antoine had only been doing this the past few weeks, Nikan figured they'd had other victims before him. They probably picked the weakest vampires they could find or those who had something to lose like Antoine, then used them up until they killed them.

"Come on." Nikan squeezed Esperanze's knee before they raced across the roof toward the door that led downstairs.

"I'm already in my vehicle. They're turning north on New York Avenue. Tell Esperanze to drive parallel to it from the east and if they turn in your direction I'll keep going straight," Thabit's voice streamed through his earpiece.

"Did you hear that?" he asked Esperanze as they slid into the rental.

"Yep." She zoomed away from the old building, her hands clasped tightly on the wheel and her jaw firmly set.

Minutes later, Thabit told them the Mercedes was heading their way and the Land Rover was following. Nikan was impressed as Esperanze fell in behind the cars, but made sure to keep a couple cars in between them. He kept Thabit apprised of their position and once they'd been following the Moretti brothers for five minutes, they turned off and let Thabit take over.

It took some slick driving, but Esperanze hadn't been exaggerating. She'd definitely memorized the layout of the city.

"Damn, woman, I'm getting turned on watching you drive like this," he said, loving seeing this side to his sweet, beta female.

Esperanze grinned even as her cheeks flushed red. When Thabit reminded them that he could hear them, they darkened even more.

After that Nikan forced his gaze to the road in front of them. When they started heading deeper into the downtown historic district, the Land Rover and Mercedes split up.

As Thabit relayed the information to them, Nikan had a split second decision to make. "Can you keep up with the Land Rover?" he asked Esperanze.

She nodded. "I can try."

"Thabit, stay with Antoine, see where he's headed. We'll follow the other guy."

"Will do. I'll call you back once we reach a destination."

As they disconnected, Esperanze took a sharp turn, running through a yellow light as she turned down a street parallel to the one Marco Moretti had turned down a block ahead of them.

"We're headed into a pretty nice neighborhood," she said.

Nikan nodded in agreement, keeping an eye out his window, watching the Land Rover move along next to them each time there was a break in buildings. As they pulled up to a light, he saw Marco turning to the right, away from them.

"He's moving east," he said.

After a quick glance to make sure they were clear, Esperanze gunned it and made another turn. Weaving in and out of vehicles, she zipped along until they were only a few cars behind the Land Rover. It was hard not to be impressed with her. She was moving smoothly, but not drawing any attention to them.

When the other vehicle pulled down a narrow, brick paved street, Nikan went with his gut. "Keep going."

"You sure?" Her fingers tightened on the wheel.

"Yeah, he'll know if we're following." It was a very residential place. Nikan figured he wasn't cutting through as a shortcut. "Turn here." He motioned to the next street. As she did, he was already gripping the handle. "Pull in behind that van."

She did as he said, but frowned when he slid out of the car. Before she could ask what he was doing, he said, "I've got his scent, I'm tracking him on foot from here. Stay put and I'll call as soon as he stops." *If he stopped.* Without waiting for a response, Nikan took off. Even in human form, he was a hell of a lot faster than humans. It might look odd for him to be sprinting through a quiet residential neighborhood, but it wasn't against the law.

Right now they couldn't afford to be seen. Luckily it was cold enough outside that there weren't any moms pushing strollers or people out jogging. The biting wind rushed over him as his feet pounded against the sidewalk. He was moving so fast that if someone glanced out their window, they'd probably question if they'd seen anything at all. He'd prefer running in wolf form but that would definitely get him noticed.

The Moretti brother he was after had a distinctive lemon undertone that was part of his natural scent. Everyone had an odor that was unique to them and Nikan was homing in on this guy faster and faster. Historic homes, bare trees and cars parked on the cobblestone streets flew by him, but when he turned down another street he spotted the Land Rover moving in his direction.

Nikan slowed and ducked behind a parked truck with an extended cab. He could hear a few muffled voices in the near vicinity, meaning some people were in their homes, but it was a very quiet day on the streets.

Peering through the slightly darkened glass of the truck's back window, he spotted Marco Moretti parking on the street then walking toward a two-story Victorian style home. He paused and glanced around, but it was a quick sweep. As he headed up the front steps, Nikan walked a little farther down the sidewalk to get a better view and watched as Marco slid a key in the front door then stepped inside.

The home was surrounded by trees and shrubbery which was probably for privacy, but it could be a very good thing for Nikan. If he needed to sneak in, he'd have a decent amount of cover.

Crossing the street, he kept his walk casual, but was hyper-aware of his surroundings. He didn't see any curtains in windows fluttering or blinds sliding up from neighbors' houses. More important he didn't hear any concerned voices or conversations. Normally he could tune out his extrasensory abilities, especially when it came to overhearing human conversations, but now he centered himself and focused on listening to the people in the surrounding area. With the fences and giant oak trees in so many of the front yards, he had a lot of cover.

The nearer he got to the Victorian home, the more he focused specifically on it.

"Don't pull my arm so hard, you're hurting me," a slightly slurred female voice said.

"Quit complaining and sit down." Definitely Marco Moretti.

Nikan glanced back at a street sign, then looked at the numbers in front of the house. This place wasn't listed as their property and it wasn't the address on his brother's license. A siren sounded in the distance, momentarily distracting him. Straining, he forced himself to focus.

"When am I going to get to see Antoine?"

"In a couple hours you two are going to be reunited." The shifter laughed, the sound harsh.

Reunited. That didn't sound good. He didn't hear anyone else inside. For a fraction of a second he contemplated calling Thabit, but didn't bother. Nikan could handle one shifter on his own. Especially one as young as Marco Moretti.

From the direction of the voices he could only guess, but it sounded like they were near the front of the house.

Right now Nikan had the victim practically in his sights. He couldn't walk away or wait for backup. Not when she was so close. And he didn't want to call Esperanze. Keeping her as far away from this danger as possible was the most important thing.

His phone buzzed in his pocket. Glancing at the ID he saw Esperanze's name. Cringing, he silenced the call then turned off his phone. She would be pissed, but better that than having her show up and put herself in harm's way.

He was doing this now.

Using the overgrown bushes and trees as cover, he used his supernatural speed to make it to the side of the house. Slat blinds covered one of the windows but there was enough space at the edge of the window that he could see into a living room. Couches, a television and a few pieces of furniture, but otherwise empty.

The distinctive lemon scent was getting stronger though. At his age, Nikan had honed his skills enough to decipher out scents and sounds. Nikan just hoped Marco Moretti wasn't as advanced and wouldn't scent him coming. Considering the shifter was only thirty, he'd have another thirty years before he should be able to completely distinguish sounds and scents to the point where he'd be a decent hunter. Too bad he probably wasn't going to live that long.

Large bushes blocked Nikan's movements from the house next door as he inched farther along the wall of the house. Stopping at another window, he peered inside. A dark haired woman with bronze skin and obvious Indian heritage sat at a kitchen table, her hands loosely tied in front of her. The binding had been done quickly, probably because the shifters didn't view her as a threat or think she'd try to escape. Or she might have been drugged considering the way she'd sounded earlier.

Moving a fraction to the right, he caught sight of Marco Moretti by the kitchen washing his hands. There was enough distance between the woman and Marco that Nikan could take him by surprise.

Before he had time to second-guess himself, he stripped out of his clothes, sprinted across the driveway and part of the yard until he was at the line of bushes. Taking a deep breath he underwent the change. Bones broke, realigned and hurt with a vengeance. Black fur sprouted where skin had been, covering him as his wolf took over. The change was always abrupt and painful, but then a rush of euphoria engulfed him. Using all his strength, he raced back the way he'd come then launched himself through the window.

Not subtle, but he needed the element of surprise. Glass and the wood frame splintered around him, shards flying everywhere as he crashed into the kitchen. The blinds were roughly tossed to the tile floor.

The woman screamed, diving out of her chair and away from him. *Good.* He didn't want her in the way.

Marco had turned at the initial crash and hadn't wasted time shifting into his wolf form. Slightly smaller and a little more wiry than Nikan, the light brown and white wolf growled in front of him on all fours, his clothes and shoes shredded on the floor.

Nikan bared his lengthened canines, growling at the other animal. Marco growled back and swiped at the air in front of him with a forepaw.

Circling to the right, Nikan kept his movements slow and measured, hoping the closer he moved toward the woman, she'd take the hint and run out behind him now that he was between her and Marco. When he heard her feet shuffling against the floor and farther away from them, he let his beast go. These bastards had taken an innocent woman for pure profit. Not to mention they were risking vamp and shifter relations. He felt no guilt attacking Marco Moretti.

Snarling, he lunged but kept his head down to protect his throat. It took a lot to kill a shifter. Beheading was one way. Ripping out the heart was the other. Both hard to do because no shifter was going to stay still and let someone kill them.

As he flew toward Marco, he felt the other shifter's claws dig into his shoulders then swipe down his back. Pain registered but adrenaline was rapidly pumping through him. And Nikan didn't mind a little blood loss. Not when he could go for the killing blow. Swiveling his head back up, he crunched down on the back of other wolf's neck.

Howling, Marco jerked back, pulling out of Nikan's hold. Cursing himself that he hadn't gotten a better grip the first time, Nikan pounced, refusing to let this drag out longer than it had to.

Swiping out with his claws, he sliced open Marco's face. Another howl emitted from the shifter, but Nikan didn't pause in his attack. He kept swiping and clawing until he had the wolf on the ground. Blood pooled all around them, spreading across the tile floor in a dark crimson. His wolf was in control now, doing what was necessary.

Without pause, he bit down, finishing what he'd started moments before. Cutting through tendon and muscle, he didn't stop until Marco's head was lying in a bloody heap next to his body.

At the sound of a terrified gasp, he turned to find the dark-haired woman standing in the entryway, her face pale as she tugged the remainder of the bindings off using her teeth. Why hadn't she run away? Before he could contemplate that, a very familiar scent drew his attention toward the broken window. Looking over he saw Esperanze peeking inside with wide eyes at the destruction and carnage.

"You couldn't have waited for me?" She started to grab the edge of the window as if to pull herself through, but there were too many glass points sticking out.

He growled at her then shifted back to his human form. Uncaring about the blood or his nudity, he shook his head. "Don't. I'll open the back door."

"Who are you people?" the woman finally asked.

"We're friends of Antoine, here to save you," Nikan said without turning toward her as he opened the back door.

Esperanze looked him over, her eyes filled with worry. She reached out as though needing to touch him, but pulled her hand back. "Are you injured? I don't want to hurt you more." Biting her bottom lip, she met his gaze. A light sheen of wetness glistened there and it took him a moment to realize it was unshed tears.

"Essie, I'm fine." Disregarding the blood on his hands and torso, he pulled her into a tight hug. His back had been slashed but as a warrior, he was already healing. In the next hour he'd be completely fine.

"You didn't answer your phone and I got worried." Her arms went around him without pause. A small shudder sped through her.

"How'd you find me?" he murmured against her hair, soaking up her sweet honeysuckle scent.

"You're not the only one who can track. I followed your stupid scent," she said.

He pulled back a fraction, but didn't lessen his hold. "Stupid?"

"Yes, right now I'm mad at you for making me worry so it's stupid." She sniffled lightly, making his guilt skyrocket, but it was tempered with the knowledge that she truly cared about him. She wouldn't be crying on his chest if she didn't. There hadn't been time to answer her call and they had other things to deal with at the moment.

"We'll talk later." Releasing his hold, he turned to face Chandra, who still stood in the doorway. "Is this where they've been holding you the entire time?"

Clearly avoiding looking at the dead body, she nodded and pointed at what he guessed was a pantry door. "That leads to a basement. It's not dingy or anything. I had a television, my own bathroom and a mini fridge, but they kept me locked in there almost 24/7."

"Did they... do you need medical attention right now?" He wasn't sure how to phrase what he wanted to ask.

Chandra frowned, then her expression cleared as she shook her head. "They didn't assault me or anything." She looked down at Marco's dead body and shuddered. "Don't get me wrong, they're both assholes and I'm not sorry he's dead, but, no, I don't need medical attention.... Where's the other one?"

Instead of answering he looked down at Esperanze. "Will you grab my phone and clothes? I left them—"

She nodded quickly. "I saw them outside."

As she disappeared out the backdoor, he turned to Chandra who was purposefully avoiding his gaze. Cringing, he looked around and grabbed a hand towel. Trying to cover himself with it, he held it up against his groin. "The other one is with Antoine right now. I need to call a colleague of mine and let him know you're safe."

"Shouldn't we call the police?"

Nikan shook his head. "No cops right now. If we involve them, they'll involve my Council and the vampire Brethren. Shifters used you to make Antoine do some illegal stuff. It won't matter to the vamps that he did it to save you. You're just a human and to them—"

She nodded, cutting him off. "I get it. And I don't mind lying to save Antoine." Her voice softened as she said the vampire's name.

Esperanze strode back through the door, Nikan's clothes and cell phone in hand. After wiping as much of the blood off himself as he could, he put his clothes back on and dialed Thabit.

From the intel his packmates had gathered, he knew the Moretti brothers didn't have any partners. Whether it was right or wrong, Nikan sure as hell didn't want to involve the authorities. They'd have to make up something for why Chandra had been gone for these last few weeks, but lying was better than pitting shifters and vamps against one another. The last thing either species needed was unnecessary tension. They had enough problems keeping peace with the humans. And once bureaucrats got involved, all semblance of peace between them would disintegrate.

Thabit picked up on the first ring. "Yeah?"

"The woman is safe and Marco is no longer a problem."

"Is that right?"

"Yep, but it's a little messy."

"Where are you?"

"A house, populated residential area." Nikan seriously doubted anyone was listening to their conversation but he kept the details as vague as possible.

"Do you need a cleanup crew?"

Nikan was surprised the lupine shifter could arrange that, but said, "Yes. Immediately."

"I'll take care of his brother. Text me the address and get out of that house. Take the human with you, but don't go back to your hotel room. Not yet. Once I'm done with the shifter, I'll meet you and pick her up."

"Then what?"

"Then you and that pretty woman of yours are going to get the hell out of town. You don't need to be involved in this anymore."

Hell yes.

Anything to get Esperanze out of there. Nikan didn't like the idea of leaving anything unfinished, but he also didn't want Esperanze in DC any longer either. After disconnecting he looked at Chandra. "Do you have any personal belongings downstairs?" Thabit might be sending a cleanup crew but he figured they could take what they could now.

She shook her head.

"Good. We're getting you the hell out of here."

Swallowing hard, the woman took a few tentative steps toward them. It was almost like whatever wall she'd had around herself cracked. Tears streamed down her face and she started to shake. "Thank you so much for saving me. I thought... I'm pretty sure they meant to kill me tonight." As she wrapped her arms around herself, Esperanze hurried to her side and slid her arm around Chandra's shoulder.

"Come on. You're never going to have to see this place or either of those bastards again," Esperanze said.

Palming the car keys, Nikan went outside and did a quick visual sweep before texting Thabit the address. From what he could see and hear, no one was aware of the violence that had just taken place.

He really hoped it stayed that way.

Chapter 13

Esperanze slowly opened her eyes, blinking away the sleep that had taken her by surprise. She looked at the clock on the dashboard of their new rental and realized they were already five hours into their almost eight-hour trip back to North Carolina. She glanced over at Nikan as he drove, sad that soon they'd be at the ranch and back to reality.

Not that her everyday life was a bad thing. She loved her pack and life on the ranch, especially since Nikan and the other warriors were now living among them.

But he hadn't said a word about their earlier conversation. Granted they hadn't had much time since meeting up with Thabit and Antoine then packing up all their stuff and getting out of town. After Nikan had spoken to Connor, they'd all made a unified decision not to involve their Council or any vampire leaders. Antoine had been more than willing to do that and Thabit had gone along with it, because if lupine shifters and vampires had gotten into a war over what had happened, feline shifters would eventually have been dragged into it as well.

So Thabit had disposed of the bodies and called in a cleanup crew to "sanitize" the house they'd found Chandra in. Esperanze didn't even want to know the details of that. And Chandra was going to tell the cops she had been held by unknown assailants in a basement for the past few weeks but managed to escape when they left the door unlocked. Once the sun had set, the plan was for her to stumble into a police station, unsure where she'd been held, just that she'd run the moment she'd escaped.

Not exactly brilliant, and they might not believe her, but Chandra still had drugs in her system when they found her so it would hopefully tie in to her story about not remembering exactly where she was being held, who had her or even why they wanted her. Esperanze was just glad she wasn't the one having to lie to the police. Either way, it was obvious Chandra was a victim and Esperanze couldn't see the cops harassing her when she had nothing to gain from lying. Especially since she was such a respected member of the academic community.

Shifting in her seat, Esperanze glanced out the window, forcing her gaze away from Nikan's defined profile. He hadn't wanted to fly home and she hadn't argued. It just meant more time spent with him. Unfortunately the longer they drove, the closer they were to the ranch and nothing had been resolved between them. Something twisted around her chest, squeezing the air out of her lungs and making it hard to breathe. She couldn't let him go.

Maybe he'd changed his mind about mating. No, she couldn't believe that. Not after what they'd been through together. As she took in the trees and road flying by, she realized they weren't on the highway anymore but a two lane winding road. There weren't many lights except the stars and half-moon. "Where are we?" Her voice sounded raspy as she spoke for the first time in hours.

"You'll see soon." Nikan's deep voice washed over her, soothing her.

"Are we making a stop before we head home?" *Please say yes.* Anything to stretch out their time together. It was almost one in the morning so he was probably tired anyway. Maybe he wanted to stop and get some sleep.

He shot her a quick look full of promise. "Do you *want* to stop?"

Unable to find her voice, she simply nodded.

Nikan didn't say anything, just turned his attention back to the road, but his earthy scent intensified with each second that passed. Yeah, he definitely still wanted her. His fingers grasped the wheel so tight his knuckles had turned white. A few minutes later he pulled off the two-lane road onto a paved driveway that stretched on for over a mile at least. He was silent so she didn't ask questions, though she couldn't quell her building curiosity.

Eventually they pulled up to a two-story log cabin. There were no lights but it was obvious the place was well maintained. The shrubs out front were covered with sheets to guard against the frost and the stone walkway leading up to the front steps had been cleared of the light layer of snow that dusted the rest of the yard and surrounding woods.

"What is this place?" she asked.

As he put the car in park, he turned to look at her. Even though she could see well in the darkness, shadows played off the angles of his face, making it difficult to read his expression. "A piece of property Connor owns—well, the pack owns now. It's available for anyone to use. We're about two hours north of Fontana."

"How long are we staying here?"

"As long as it takes."

She thought she knew what he meant but didn't want to get too excited. "What takes?"

Reaching out, he ran his knuckles across her cheek before cupping her jaw. "To convince you to mate with me."

It felt as if her heart skipped a beat though she knew that was impossible. Her throat seized for a moment as she digested what he was telling her. "You really want to mate? You weren't just being all alpha with Thabit?" He growled and she raised her eyebrows. "What's that for?"

His expression was dark, almost feral. "I don't like you saying his name."

She grinned despite his serious expression. "Oh really?"

"The only name I want on your lips is mine. Over and over as you come."

Feeling her face flush, she swallowed hard. She loved it when he talked like that. It made her nipples tingle and warmth flood the juncture between her thighs. "First you've got to *make* me come."

A shudder rolled through him as his hand slightly tightened against her face. He surprised her when he let it drop. He reached into his jacket pocket and handed her a single key on a silver key ring in the shape of a wolf howling at the moon. "Go inside." His words were practically an order.

"What?"

"Now, before I take you right here in the front seat of this car. I'll bring in our bags."

She inwardly smiled at the knowledge he was losing control. That's what she wanted from this man. The man she definitely wanted as her mate. She opened the door and nearly shivered as the cold rolled inside. "Well you'd better hurry or I might make you wait longer to mark me."

His dark eyes widened and his head slightly tilted to the side. "You mean..."

She slid out of the car and raced for the front door. Behind her she could hear his boots pounding against the walkway. Looked like he'd decided not to get their bags after all. She'd never thought she'd want a man to chase her, but right now the feeling of being hunted by a man as powerful as Nikan sent a thrill up her spine.

Esperanze had barely slid the key in the door when he reached her. His massive hands clasped her shoulders. Spinning her around, he pulled her tight against his body, his hands sliding down to cup her butt as he pressed her pelvis to his. He was rock hard and even though she was a little nervous, she couldn't wait to feel him inside her.

Her entire body ached for this. She'd known for a while that her feelings for him went well past friendship, but she'd been too afraid to admit it out loud.

This weekend had proved to her that he viewed her as an equal. They might be physically different, but that didn't matter. He valued her in every way that mattered and she couldn't get enough of him. She wanted to be his forever.

One hand tightened on her as one moved away. She heard the door swing open behind them, but he didn't take his gaze off her. He was breathing hard as he stared down at her. "I'm playing for keeps, Essie. I want you for my mate and eventually my bond-mate."

At the word bondmate, she slightly jerked back, but he just tightened his hold. When they mated they'd be linked, much like humans who married. Other supernatural beings would know they were off limits but if they eventually wanted to part ways they could. It would be the equivalent of humans divorcing one another.

That couldn't happen if they were bonded. It wasn't as if they could bond tonight anyway. They could only do that under the full moon. His admission honored her, yes, but it still stunned her. "Nikan..." She didn't know how to respond.

"I don't need you to say anything. I'm just telling you how I feel. I love you, Essie. Have for a while. I want to live with you, have kids with you—"

Her heart swelled at his words and she couldn't keep her own feelings in any longer. "I love you too." Reaching up she clasped his face between her hands. "I want to be your mate, I want to feel you inside me tonight and tomorrow and—"

Her words were lost as his mouth crushed over hers. His tongue invaded her mouth, frantic and hungry as his hands grasped her behind, hoisting her up so that she had no choice but to wrap her legs around his waist.

Feeling his erection press against her, she moaned and gripped his shoulders. She was vaguely aware of them moving inside and the front door shutting behind them.

Nikan was walking them somewhere. She didn't care where as long as it was a flat surface. The wall, floor, a couch, it didn't matter as long as he was inside her.

For a brief moment she felt as if she was falling. Her eyes snapped open and she pulled back just as her arms collided with something soft. Twisting to the side she realized he'd laid her on a giant pile of blankets in a living room. Right in front of a fireplace.

He stood as she propped up on her elbows, already missing his warmth. "What are you doing?"

His expression was dark, almost feral and she could tell he was struggling with control. "Give me just a second..." He turned away and felt along the wall by the fireplace. "I had Connor call the caretaker and make sure this place was set up for us." He flipped a switch and a fire flared to life in the stone fireplace.

She blinked, trying to figure out how he'd done it when she realized it was gas and the log set and fire must be fake. The heat was real though. But she didn't care about any of that. She only cared about the very sexy man staring at her as if she was the most precious thing in the world.

When he crouched down on his knees in front of her she didn't make a move toward him. First she wanted to see what she'd been fantasizing about for too long. She'd seen him naked in that house but it hadn't been the time or the place to stare. "Take off your sweater," she ordered.

His eyebrows raised. "That sounds like a demand."

"It is."

Nikan's lips quirked up at the corners. He grasped the hem of his sweater and tugged upward until she got the perfect view of his chest. A few scars nicked the sharp planes of all those muscles. They only added to his raw sexiness. She wanted to run her fingers then mouth over every single one. Mesmerized, she raked her gaze over his bronze skin, drinking in her fill while the firelight flickered around him. She might have seen his chest in the hotel room too, but now she wanted everything.

"Now the pants," she whispered.

His long fingers played with the button of his dark, well-worn jeans until he finally slid it out of the hole. She let out a breath she hadn't realized she'd been holding. But then he suddenly stopped.

"What are you doing?" she demanded, needing to see all of him.

Grinning, he reached for her. Sliding one of her pant legs up, he unzipped her boot and slid it off. "If I get naked, I'm going to be on you, then in you. Let me give you some foreplay, Essie," he softly growled.

"I *guess* I can deal with that." She couldn't bite back her smile.

His gaze flicked to hers again. "I love it when you get feisty."

"Really?"

He slid her other boot off then quickly followed with her thin socks. "*Really*. I like that you don't hold back, that you're not afraid to be yourself with me."

How did he say exactly the right thing? Only she knew he wasn't paying her lip service. He was being completely serious. Something she loved about him. He only said what he meant. No bullshit from Nikan Lawless. Something she should have realized earlier. He wouldn't have said he wanted to mate with her without being absolutely sure.

As he started unbuttoning her pants and sliding them down her legs she reached for the tie on her wraparound sweater and pulled the bow free. Her top fell open, revealing the lacy purple bra she'd worn for Nikan. It was purely for show. Tiny crystals meant to look like diamonds dotted around the demi-cups, drawing the eye directly to the rounded curves of her breasts.

His hands froze at her knees as he stared at her. His gaze cut a scorching path down her stomach to the matching lace thong. He wouldn't know the skimpy cut until she turned over, but the front was a sheer, tiny triangle, leaving very little to the imagination. Watching him watch her so intently made a slow burning heat build inside her.

"Do you wear sexy stuff like this all the time?" he rasped out, hunger in his voice and in his dark eyes.

She couldn't help it. She laughed at his very male question. The sound seemed to jerk him out of his daze.

He looked back at her face, his expression apologetic. "Sorry. I just meant... you look beautiful."

Just like that he was back in action, tugging her pants the rest of the way off. While he moved she did the same, slipping her sweater off. She'd never felt so exposed before, but she'd also never felt so wanted.

The way he devoured her with his eyes, without him saying a word, she could clearly see how much he not only desired her but how much he treasured her.

Now that she was almost completely bared to him she didn't know what to do with her hands. Nerves hummed through her with a vengeance. She sat up fully and started to cover herself but he clasped her wrists and pushed her flat on her back. Stretching out on top of her, he covered her body with his, loosely holding her wrists above her head.

"You don't get to cover yourself around me anymore, Essie. You're mine." He nipped her jaw, raking his teeth along her skin.

His words set off an explosion inside her. Arching her back, she rubbed her covered breasts against his chest. They felt swollen, the tips aching for his touch.

Still holding her wrists with one hand, Nikan reached between their bodies and cupped one of her breasts. "Mine," he murmured against her mouth as he gently squeezed.

Pulling one of her hands free she reached between them and grasped his cock over his jeans. "Mine."

"Hell yeah it's yours, sweetheart." He playfully tugged her bottom lip between his teeth. Letting her other wrist go, he moved lower until his face was right over her breasts.

He stared for a long moment, his breathing unsteady, until finally he unsnapped the front clasp of her bra. As it fell apart to completely expose her she had to resist the urge to cover up.

Any insecurities she had died at the look on his face. He let out a low, primal growl before sucking one of her nipples into his mouth. She gasped at the warmth surrounding her aching flesh, feeling the erotic tug all the way to her toes. Spreading her legs wider, she wrapped them around him, rubbing herself against his covered erection as he teased her sensitive flesh.

Each time he stroked one of her nipples with his tongue, he followed up by softly blowing on it. The hot air on her wet flesh made her shudder and arch into him each time.

She was already so wet she knew that once he finally got inside her it wouldn't take long for her to come. Her inner walls clenched with the need to feel him. A raw urgency hummed through her as she imagined what it would feel like to come around his fingers again.

As if he read her thoughts, he reached down and cupped her through her skimpy covering. Using the same skilled movements he had at that club, he shoved the material to the side and slid one, then two fingers inside her. He began stroking in and out of her, slow and steady and not fast enough for her to reach climax.

Writhing against him, she rolled her hips, trying to make him move faster, to find that same rhythm he'd made her climax with before.

He just laughed softly against her breast. The sensation made her shiver. *He knows exactly how much he's teasing me.*

Continuing to slowly push inside her then withdraw with an equally frustrating rhythm, he moved away from her breasts, kissing and nipping a path down her belly until he was crouched directly between her legs.

Though her instinct was to tense up under such intense scrutiny, she let her thighs fall farther apart and watched him. Every part of her being trusted this man. He was just as entranced as she was, staring at his fingers moving in and out of her.

"I've fantasized about this from the *moment* I saw you." The low-spoken words seemed to be torn from him.

She looked up to meet his gaze which had turned molten hot. His dark eyes seemed to practically glow with need. She opened her mouth to respond but no words came out because in the next instant his mouth was fully on her exposed sex.

Her hips rolled up to meet his face as pleasure swamped her senses. She heard a slight tearing sound and it registered that he'd ripped her thong off. She didn't mind.

As his tongue delved inside her she grasped his head with her hands. Threading her fingers through his thick hair, she didn't bite back her moans. With each long stroke he ended on her clit, circling and putting just the right amount of pressure on the sensitive area that she kept jolting off of the soft blankets.

His fingers were still moving inside her and it was all she could do to think straight. Pleasure shot through her body, firing up all her senses as a sharp climax tore through her. She'd known she was close, but it punched through her hard and fast, taking her slightly off guard.

Afraid she might claw him she grasped the blanket beneath her as he continued his delicious assault on her. As she was coming down from her high he grasped her hips and flipped her over before she could attempt to catch her breath. She heard the soft buzz of his zipper and then the sound of his jeans being shoved down.

In a long, slow thrust he pushed inside her. Her breath caught in her throat and she arched her back. He stretched her, filling her more than she'd imagined. Her fingers dug into the blankets at the sheer pleasure of knowing that Nikan was claiming her. That they would soon be linked.

Then he began moving and there was nothing steady about his movements. Nothing rhythmic. He pumped into her in jerky, uncontrolled movements. One of his hands palmed her stomach and he moved lower until he strummed her swollen clit.

She should have been too sated, but the feel of his callused finger rubbing her already sensitized bundle of nerves made her clench even tighter around him. With each stroke of his cock and each flick of his finger, her inner walls clenched, milking him until he let out a harsh cry.

As he came inside her he wrapped a strong arm around her waist and pulled her back until his mouth was on her neck. She knew what was coming and tensed in anticipation.

Yes. Do it.

His canines pierced her neck, sharp and bordering on painful, but it only increased the intensity of her orgasm. She cried out his name. More pleasure surged through her, like a never ending wave until finally her arms and legs were too limp to hold herself up anymore.

Before she collapsed, Nikan wrapped an arm around her and held her up so that her back was pressed against his chest. He flicked his tongue over where he'd bitten her, licking and nuzzling the mark with an incredible gentleness, sending little sparks of sensation cascading over her skin. "I love you, Essie." It was a bare whisper on his lips.

She smiled, loving to hear him say it and knowing she'd never get tired of it. "I love you too."

Rolling her over, he gently laid her down, then finished shoving the rest of his clothes off. She knew better than to laugh at the moment but it struck her as completely adorable that he hadn't even been able to take off his clothes before making love to her.

As he stretched out next to her he gathered her close, pulling her so that she was halfway covering him. Her long hair fell down her back and over his body, covering them both and creating a little cocoon around them. In that moment she'd never felt more relaxed or at peace with the world.

His hand idly stroked down her spine, his breathing somewhat under control now. But the raw energy humming through him told her that she was in for a long, delicious night. Reaching up, she gently rubbed the tender spot where he'd marked her. Now all shifters and other supernatural beings would know she was off limits. Taken. Mated. She smiled in satisfaction.

His earthy scent twined around her and would remain there as long they were together. It was the same for him. Her scent was practically embedded in his skin. There wasn't a science to it; it's just the way it happened when shifters mated.

If they split up the mark would eventually fade and they'd be free to move on with someone else, but she knew there was no one else for her. He'd scared her a little with his talk of bonding, but deep in her heart she knew there would never be any other option. She wanted to eventually bond with him, to wear his mark permanently. "So what happens when we make it back to the ranch?"

He paused for a long moment but finally said, "I'd like to move in with you and your sisters. Eventually I'd like to build us a home on the ranch, but for now I don't think your sisters could handle you moving out, and I love your family."

Something tightened around her chest. He wasn't just saying that because he thought she needed to hear it. He meant it. Her sisters adored him and while it would take some adjusting to having a male under their roof all the time, she didn't think it would be that big of a difference considering how much time he'd been spending with them anyway.

"That sounds perfect." And it did. She couldn't wait to tell her sisters. Alicia's death had hit them all so hard. Having Nikan close would probably go a long way in making them feel safer. But for her, the idea of waking up to him every morning was absolute perfection. There wouldn't be a full moon for over a month and she planned to tell Nikan she wanted him for her bondmate. Not yet, but very soon. Right now the idea of talking felt highly overrated. As his hand slid down her back and cupped her behind in a possessive manner that had quickly become familiar, she grinned against the hard wall of his chest.

Talking could definitely wait.

Epilogue

Two days later

Nikan shut the front door of the cabin behind him as he stepped inside. Just as a precaution he'd been checking the direct perimeter of the house and the extended surrounding area the past couple days. There were no tracks or scents that didn't belong.

The sweet scent of Esperanze pervaded the air, wrapping around him as he strode toward the kitchen. He paused when his cell phone buzzed in his jacket pocket. When he saw Connor's name on the caller ID, a slight chill slid through his veins. His Alpha had agreed to give them a few days alone. He wouldn't be calling if it wasn't important. Not after Nikan had told Connor that he and Esperanze had mated.

He answered his phone. "Yeah?"

"I hate to do this, but I need you back now." There was no room for argument in his Alpha's voice.

Nikan's hand fisted around the phone as he entered the kitchen. Esperanze paused from making sandwiches, no doubt because of the grim look he knew was on his face. "What's happened?"

Connor sighed. "Nothing. *Yet.* Liam's getting more agitated watching over December. She's ignoring him, but that hasn't stopped him from looking out for her. I received a 'friendly' warning call from her brother telling me to rein Liam in."

Everyone at the ranch knew how bad Liam had it for December, a human female. Unfortunately her brother was the sheriff of Fontana, and he wasn't exactly a fan of shifters. And Liam wasn't being subtle about his intentions toward the sheriff's sister. That whole situation was just a bomb waiting to go off.

With a violent element, the Antiparanormal League, in town and targeting humans sympathetic to the shifters in Fontana, their pack had to be on high alert at all times. Especially now. Their pack couldn't afford for any humans to get hurt because of their association with them—definitely not the sheriff's sister.

That would cause bad blood among the rest of the town. Not to mention Liam would go insane if anything happened to the human woman he so obviously cared for.

Something Nikan understood completely.

But if Liam pissed off December's brother bad enough, that could cause even more unnecessary problems for the pack. They definitely didn't need to tangle with local law enforcement.

Before Nikan could respond, Connor continued. "I need more round the clock monitoring of the ranch *and* for December. Liam's killing himself trying to watch her 24/7 and *fuck*, he needs to sleep sometime. He's too edgy and sleep-deprived and I'm worried about him." The sharp curse from Connor didn't surprise Nikan. Liam might be more than a century old, but he was also Connor's younger brother.

Nikan didn't need to hear anymore. He might want more alone time with Essie, but his pack was his family and he knew she felt the same way. "We're on our way." At his words, Esperanze began gathering the foodstuff.

It didn't take long to pack what little they'd brought and put their suitcases in the vehicle. Less than ten minutes later they were on the road, heading back to the real world.

"I wish we could stay longer," Esperanze said as they pulled onto the main highway.

He snorted. "Me too." Two days wasn't nearly long enough to spend naked with her. They'd gotten a few runs in and had actually eaten a few meals, but other than that, he'd spent most of his time inside her. The more times he took her, the more he wanted her.

It was like a never-ending hunger to claim and cherish her that he wondered if he'd ever feel a sense of normalcy around her again. Or if the driving need to mate and to protect her would always be at the forefront of his brain. At the moment he didn't really care. Not so long as she was with him.

Even though the future had a lot of unknowns—especially with the Antiparanormal League lurking around Fontana—right now he was truly happy for the first time in as long as he could remember. It was all because of the sweet woman sitting next to him. The woman he planned to bond with and spend a lifetime loving.

Unfortunately he had a feeling things were about to drastically change in Fontana. Things couldn't keep going the way they were. The Antiparanormal League wasn't going to stay quiet forever. Eventually they'd make a move against his pack. It was just a matter of when and how. He knew his pack and his Alpha well enough that if some radical hate group pushed them hard enough, they'd push back. And the outcome would be bloody.

About the Author

Katie Reus is the *USA Today* bestselling author of the Red Stone Security series, the Ancients Rising series and the Redemption Harbor series. She fell in love with romance at a young age thanks to books she pilfered from her mom's stash. Years later she loves reading romance almost as much as she loves writing it.

However, she didn't always know she wanted to be a writer. After changing majors many times, she finally graduated summa cum laude with a degree in psychology. Not long after that she discovered a new love. Writing. She now spends her days writing paranormal romance and sexy romantic suspense. If you would like to be notified of future releases, please visit her website: https://katiereus.com and join her newsletter.

Complete Booklist

Ancients Rising

Ancient Protector

Ancient Enemy

Ancient Enforcer

Ancient Vendetta

Ancient Retribution

Ancient Vengeance

Ancient Sentinel

Ancient Warrior

Ancient Guardian

Darkness Series

Darkness Awakened

Taste of Darkness

Beyond the Darkness

Hunted by Darkness

Into the Darkness

Saved by Darkness

Guardian of Darkness

Sentinel of Darkness

A Very Dragon Christmas

Darkness Rising

Deadly Ops Series

Targeted

Bound to Danger

Chasing Danger

Shattered Duty

Edge of Danger

A Covert Affair

Endgame Trilogy

Bishop's Knight

Bishop's Queen

Bishop's Endgame

Holiday With a Hitman Series

How the Hitman Stole Christmas

MacArthur Family Series

Falling for Irish

Unintended Target

Saving Sienna

Moon Shifter Series

Alpha Instinct

Lover's Instinct

Primal Possession

Mating Instinct

His Untamed Desire

Avenger's Heat

Hunter Reborn

Protective Instinct

Dark Protector

A Mate for Christmas

O'Connor Family Series

Merry Christmas, Baby

Tease Me, Baby

It's Me Again, Baby

Mistletoe Me, Baby

Red Stone Security Series®

No One to Trust

Danger Next Door

Fatal Deception

Miami, Mistletoe & Murder

His to Protect

Breaking Her Rules

Protecting His Witness

Sinful Seduction

Under His Protection

Deadly Fallout

Sworn to Protect

Secret Obsession

Love Thy Enemy

Dangerous Protector

Lethal Game

Secret Enemy

Saving Danger

Guarding Her

Deadly Protector

Danger Rising

Protecting Rebel

Redemption Harbor® Series

Resurrection

Savage Rising

Dangerous Witness

Innocent Target

Hunting Danger

Covert Games

Chasing Vengeance

Redemption Harbor® Security

Fighting for Hailey

Fighting for Reese

Fighting for Adalyn

Made in the USA
Columbia, SC
23 January 2024

29921512R00071